"You get to b **boy."**

Cole's eyes lit up.

"Exactly like the s

"Me?"

Emma almost wished she hadn't caught the radiant glow in Jake's eyes before she replied, "Yep, you. What do you think of that?"

Cole's adorable grin gave her all the answer she needed.

"That's great. Isn't it, Cole?" Jake was touched even more than she'd expected him to be.

"I get to be in the manger scene!" Cole declared.

"We wanted to give you a big happy memory this Christmas." Emma waited for any signs of sadness to cross the child's face, but he seemed to be able to stay in the happiness of this moment.

"We could use a few of those," Jake agreed.

"I know," she said quietly as Cole gleefully finished off his cookie. She couldn't ever hope to reduce the sadness of this first Christmas without his parents. But she was doing all she could to give him a few happy memories. That, at least, was within her reach. And Jake's, too, if she could remind him.

Allie Pleiter, an award-winning author and RITA® Award finalist, writes both fiction and nonfiction. Her passion for knitting shows up in many of her books and all over her life. Entirely too fond of French macarons and lemon meringue pie, Allie spends her days writing books and avoiding housework. Allie grew up in Connecticut, holds a BS in speech from Northwestern University and lives near Chicago, Illinois.

Books by Allie Pleiter

Love Inspired

Wander Canyon

Their Wander Canyon Wish
Winning Back Her Heart
His Christmas Wish

Matrimony Valley

His Surprise Son
Snowbound with the Best Man
Wander Canyon Courtship

Blue Thorn Ranch

The Texas Rancher's Return
Coming Home to Texas
The Texan's Second Chance
The Bull Rider's Homecoming
The Texas Rancher's New Family

Visit the Author Profile page at Harlequin.com for more titles.

His Christmas Wish

Allie Pleiter

LOVE INSPIRED

INSPIRATIONAL ROMANCE

LOVE INSPIRED®

INSPIRATIONAL ROMANCE

Recycling programs for this product may not exist in your area.

ISBN-13: 978-1-335-48850-3

His Christmas Wish

This edition published by arrangement with Harlequin Books S.A.

For questions and comments about the quality of this book, please contact us at CustomerService@Harlequin.com.

Love Inspired
22 Adelaide St. West, 40th Floor
Toronto, Ontario M5H 4E3, Canada
www.Harlequin.com

Printed in U.S.A.

I will lead them in paths that they have not known: I will make darkness light before them, and crooked things straight. These things will I do unto them, and not forsake them.
—*Isaiah* 42:16

To my new "writing partner," Paisley

Furry four-legged proof that God
always sees around corners and
can craft beautiful endings to sad stories

Chapter One

*"C*an I have four turtles? So they don't get lonely?"

Emma Mullins smiled to herself as she stood in the pet store aisle. Was a little boy pleading to get pet turtles for Christmas next month? The hopeful voice from the adjacent aisle warmed her heart—until she recognized that it belonged to Cole Wilson.

"You can have a dozen if you want, buddy," came an older voice she identified as Jake Sanders's, the boy's bachelor uncle. "With the best bowl in the whole shop."

She felt her heart pinch the way it had each time she looked at Cole. No one in Wander Canyon would deny the poor boy any bit of happiness. It was almost the holiday season and such an awful thing had happened to him. Still, Emma wasn't sure a dozen turtles was the smart path out of the little boy's sadness. Jake was charming, heartbreakingly handsome, prone to a bit of swagger—and not at all emergency parent material. She had to help. Emma set down the bag of food she was buying for the class guinea pig and made her way to the next aisle.

Jake crouched next to his nephew. It was rather sweet how the man folded his tall, athletic frame down to peer with the boy into a tank holding several dozen small green turtles. Emma had met Jake at preschool functions—he was the sort of man who stood out in any room, even a preschool classroom, and was prone to grand gestures. Emma had no doubt Jake would have indeed bought the store's entire stock to please his nephew. Especially now.

"Twelve might be a bit much," she offered with her most helpful smile. "Two might be a better start."

"Miss Emma!" the boy cried, running up to her and giving her a sweet hug. How he managed to retain any joy, despite the recent accident that killed both his parents, she might never know. The whole sorry situation made a lump rise in her throat whenever she thought of it. For a five-year-old to lose both parents on the cusp of the holidays seemed beyond tragic.

Jake stood up to meet her gaze. The defiant weariness in his eyes still didn't overshadow how handsome the man was. And yet he looked deeply sad. After all, he was grieving the loss of his sister as Cole grieved the loss of his mom. That was a steep hill to climb on any day, much less while caring for his nephew.

A free-spirited bachelor with no parenting experience, he was barely holding it together after the tragic overpass shooting that had killed Kurt and Natalie Wilson. He'd been late to pick Cole up multiple times and forgotten the boy's backpack twice. Emma hadn't yet decided if it was loving bravery or foolish pride that drove the man to step in and care for the boy while Cole's paternal grandmother traveled back to her Arizona home to make arrangements to move here to Wander Canyon. She had to admit, she rather admired Jake either way.

Emma knew better than to ask either of them how they were. So many people had drowned her family in that useless question after Mom had died. There was never a safe way to answer truthfully. While everyone meant to show concern, no one ever really wanted to hear "awful," "beyond sad," "angry" or any of the other feelings such deep grief created.

So maybe turtles weren't a bad call, after all. Unusual, perhaps, but then again so was Jake.

"So you're finally getting a turtle—or two?" Emma asked, looking up at Jake on that last word to reinforce her hint that a pair would suffice.

"Uncle Jake said I could." The little boy—whose turtle backpack and frequent drawings in school displayed a love of turtles—beamed with the broadest smile she'd seen from him in days.

Jake gave her a forlorn, *what can I do?* shrug. "Figured there was no point in waiting for Christmas." Clearly Jake knew what she did: Cole had asked many times for a pet turtle but his mother, Natalie, had been against it. Natalie was a careful, safety-conscious mother who had read up on the animals and decided against it because of the risk of disease some thought turtles carried. Who could blame Jake for reaching for any silver lining he could find right now?

"Wanna help?" Cole asked.

And who could refuse the boy? "Of course I'll help."

Cole peered into the tank, giving a wide yawn as he did. "I been up all night waiting."

That might explain Jake's weary expression—and the enormous cup of coffee in the man's hand. "Me, too." Not by choice, Emma could tell.

"When I had a scary dream in the middle of the night, Uncle Jake told me I could have a turtle."

"A great idea," Jake admitted, yawning himself. "But maybe not at four thirty in the morning."

"I was so happy, I couldn't sleep after that," Cole explained.

"Yeah," Jake said, still yawning. "Neither could I." A tiny hint of the man's high-voltage smile returned at the jest.

"Do you know stuff about turtles?" Cole asked. "Should I name him Otto? Does he need lots of friends?"

"How about just one friend," Jake suggested, raising an eyebrow in Emma's direction. "That way they can be *best* friends." He leaned in toward Emma as Cole continued peering into the tank, deciding which to choose. "Any idea how to tell the boy turtles from the girl turtles? I'd prefer to avoid hosting a turtle romance."

There, in that jaunty whisper, was the Jake Sanders most people talked about. Charming, quick with a flirty remark and never one to avoid romance of the human variety. Jake had always struck her as the sort of wild uncle who would take his nephew out for late-night ice cream and introduce him to the virtues of cold pizza for breakfast. Cole adored him, but Emma had doubts Jake was the kind of man equipped to guide Cole through his first holidays without his mother and father.

The reptilian buddies of choice turned out to be two four-inch red-eared sliders—a name that amused Cole to no end. Otto and Oscar quickly gained a spiffy little habitat with rocks, a pair of tiny plastic palm trees and a little warming lamp. As for supplies, the shop owner offered turtle pellets for food as well as a list of fruits and vegetables suitable for Otto's and Oscar's diet.

"They have to eat vegetables, too?" Cole asked in surprise, making Emma smile. "Like Mom makes…" The little boy clamped his mouth shut and looked down at the pet shop floor.

How many times had life skidded to a stop for the little boy as something else reminded him of all he had lost? Jake lost any remnant of his trademark cavalier bearing. Instead he looked up at the ceiling as grief and helplessness flashed across his strong features. The whole situation was so relentlessly sad. Random overpass shootings weren't supposed to happen out here in the mountains. They weren't supposed to happen at all. And for something so senseless to rob a little boy of his parents just before the holidays? No one—least of all Jake—seemed to know how to begin to cope.

The little boy's instant sadness made the shop owner recognize his customers. "You're Jake Sanders. Is this your nephew? The Wilson boy?" he asked with a compassionate smile.

"Yep." Emma could hear Jake trying to hide the choke in his voice. The effort doubled the size of the lump in her own throat.

The pet store owner leaned down. "That's a fine pair of turtles you picked out there, son. I'd be pleased if you'd let me give you the whole setup on the house. Bit of happiness could go a long way right now, I suppose."

Emma watched that show of support hit Jake. He stuffed his hands into his pockets, fighting the weight of the pity even as he forced a practiced smile. "Thanks." He pushed the single word out, not quite able to say more.

Emma stepped in to cover Jake's awkward moment. "That's very kind of you, Walt. What a thoughtful thing to do."

After they'd packed up the two turtles and their equipment, Emma walked with Jake and Cole toward the store exit. "I don't suppose you'd want to…um…get a post-turtle coffee or something?" Jake asked. He shook his large foam cup to display its empty status. "I need more caffeine."

Jake was clearly in need of company, and in any other circumstance he'd be pleasant company indeed—but he was now essentially the guardian of a student. If Emma wanted to keep her name at the top of the candidate list for the new preschool director when Zosia Jagoda retired, she'd best keep her professional margins wide and clear. Helping purchase bereavement turtles was one thing, but social coffees with a man of Jake's dating reputation could be seen as quite another. "I need to go back in and finish getting Zippy's food."

"He's our class guinea pig," Cole explained to Jake.

"I figured," Jake replied.

"And you need to get Oscar and Otto home, I expect," Emma added.

"We named him Zippy, but he mostly sleeps a lot. And chews." Cole peered again at the clear plastic container Jake held. "Do turtles have nap times? I think their eyes are closed."

"Can uncles have nap times?" Jake asked, yawning again.

Emma laughed. It might have actually been fun to have coffee with him, even under these circumstances. But that wasn't a smart choice. "That nap might do you better than a second quart of coffee."

"But it's not half as likely." He managed an echo of his former grin. There was a reason that smile had won more than a few hearts in Wander Canyon. "See you at drop-off Monday, then?"

Emma touched Cole's shoulder, focusing on the sweet

blue eyes of the boy rather than the alluring smoky gray ones of the man. "I'll see you then. And you can tell me all about Otto and Oscar's first nights in their new home."

"I will," Cole said, head bobbing. He cocked his head up toward his uncle. "And we won't be late again, will we, Uncle Jake?"

Ah, the blatant honesty of children. Emma couldn't help but raise an eyebrow to Jake at Cole's chiding. They'd not only been the last to arrive every day this week, but Jake had been the last parent to show up for pickup. Twice.

Jake cleared his throat at the pint-size reprimand. "We'll put in the effort. Results may vary."

Get back soon, Grandma Sarah, Emma thought as she watched Jake walk away with Cole and his new turtle buddies. *I don't think he'll last long.*

Monday morning, Jake scowled at his watch as he finished sinking a screw on a set of built-in shelves. "It can't be eleven fifteen already."

His business partner, Bo Carter, looked up from the baseboard he was nailing into place. "Time flies when you're having fun?"

Groaning, Jake set his screwdriver down. He hadn't gotten nearly as far on this project this morning as he'd hoped. Granted, the chaos of his life was wreaking havoc with his focus, but there just wasn't enough time to do anything these days. This week was looking like it would be just as bad as last week. "More like time flies when your nephew is in preschool."

"Gotta go, huh?"

"Yep." Jake was sure he'd never be able to repay Bo for how amazingly supportive his business partner had been. It bugged him to leave Bo doing the lion's share of the work, day after day. He knew he'd do the same in a heartbeat for Bo, but that didn't squelch the burn of frustration that had settled in his gut and refused to go away. "I'm really sorry." He was. Not that regret finished bookshelves or ran conduit wire or taped up drywall.

"Hey, that's what partners are for."

"I still hate leaving you like this. We're not going to start the Thompson project on time if this keeps up." Car-San Construction was a two-man operation, and he needed to be one of those two men soon. *Get on back here, Sarah*, he pleaded in his head for the hundredth time. *I'm not cut out for this.*

"We'll make it work," Bo assured him. "We always do."

"How about I bring Cole to the office after lunch and knock off a few of those estimates?" A job site was a dangerous place for a five-year-old, but there were enough ways to keep Cole occupied in the Car-San office that at least Jake could be of some use there. Still, it was killing Jake to feel as if he was doing everything halfway. Not even halfway.

"That'd help," Bo conceded. "But don't put yourself out. We got time."

More like time has me. Over a barrel. "Natalie did so much stuff. How did she get it all done with Cole underfoot all the time? I'm living my life in ten-minute attention spans." After getting Otto and Oscar settled, followed by lunch and then way too many games of Chutes and Ladders, Jake had managed to convince Cole to lie down on the couch with him Saturday afternoon and be quiet—for seventeen minutes. Sunday after church hadn't gone any better. Weren't kids supposed to need more sleep than adults? Jake felt like he could sleep seventeen hours and still not catch enough winks to keep up with his nonstop nephew.

The complaint stung Jake's heart even as he thought it. Natalie would give anything to be bothered by Cole for even one more day. Heaven was supposed to be the place of "no more tears," but Jake couldn't figure out how any young mother like Natalie could stand to be in paradise while her baby was left down on Earth. She and Kurt should be here with Cole, not him. With all the horrible people in the world, why should a random shot fired onto the highway from an overpass cut *their* lives short? Why should innocent Cole be left without a mom and dad? With Christmas just weeks away? The whole thing seemed so incredibly, painfully unjust. *Wrong, wrong, wrong.*

Bo walked over and put his hand on Jake's shoulder. "Give yourself a break. The memorial service was only two weeks ago." They'd been through a lot together in the past ten years, not the least of which was Bo's reunion and recent marriage to his high school sweetheart, Toni. "You've got a lot on your plate. Don't forget all the times you've covered for me. That's how this works."

It wasn't working. Or at least it didn't feel like it was. Jake would never classify himself as a control freak, but the nonstop sensation of life spinning out of control was getting to him. He couldn't really grieve the huge loss of his sister—he didn't have a spare moment to do it. He didn't have a spare moment to do *anything*. And now, if he didn't leave in the next five minutes, he was going to be late picking Cole up from preschool.

"Maybe. In any case, I gotta go. I'll come back after lunch."

Jake turned toward the door, only to have his cell phone ring. He figured the call could wait until pickup had been achieved...until he saw Sarah's name on the screen. Maybe Cole's grandmother was calling to say she'd wrapped things up in Arizona early and was on her way back. That'd be welcome news. "Hi, Sarah," he answered, tapping the icon to put his cell phone on speaker so he could talk as he walked toward his truck.

"Is this Jake?" A strange voice greeted him.

"Sure is. Sarah?"

"This isn't Sarah. This is her next-door neighbor, Dorothy. I'm with Sarah at the emergency room."

Jake's stomach dropped. "Everything okay?" It was a foolish question given the tone of Dorothy's voice. The words *emergency room* and *okay* never went together in his experience.

"I'm afraid not. Sarah took a fall."

Jake stilled as he opened the truck door. This did not sound anything close to okay. "Bad fall?"

"Nasty," Dorothy said. "She'll have a whopper of a bruise, but it's the ankle we're worried about. She's in getting X-rays now, but if you ask me, it's broken. Badly. Sarah told me I needed to get in touch with you right away. Honestly, if I hadn't been out walking my dog, I don't know how long she'd have been out there on her side deck."

Grandma Sarah would not be arriving early. As a matter of fact, it looked like Grandma Sarah would not be arriving anytime soon. "I'm sorry to hear that." Now, there was an understatement. He liked Natalie's mother-in-law and was sorry to hear of her accident. But he was doubly sorry that it would leave him dealing with the consequences.

It wasn't a question of *if* he would—of course, he'd do whatever Cole needed. It was more a question of *how*. A sinking sensation pushed him down as he slid onto the truck seat even as he forced steadiness into his voice and said, "You tell Sarah not to worry about us over here. Cole and I will hold down the fort until she's back on her feet."

"She feels terrible," Dorothy said. "I've been helping her pack for the move and she's so sad. It's barely been five years since Gerry left her a widow. It's just wrong how much you all have gone through. And now this."

And now this. Life had been a continual roller coaster of *and now this* lately. No one would ever call him a family man, but even Jake couldn't imagine what it was like to bury both your husband and your son in the space of five years. Sarah shouldn't be made to feel as if she was letting him down. "We'll be okay. You tell her that. And make sure Sarah gets that ankle taken care of. We can wait until she's back on her feet for her to come back to Wander."

Can we? He really didn't know the answer to that.

"How are you doing, Jake?" Dorothy's tone softened. "Sarah tells me a lot of this is falling on you. I'm so sorry about your sister."

Jake had yet to come up with a way to answer the "How are you?" question. The onslaught of *I'm so sorry*s. People meant well, but he was drowning in well-intentioned questions. People checking in on him. Cards and casseroles and "call me if you need anything"s. *Terrible, that's how I am, and there's nothing you or anyone can do.* No matter how true, it never felt like it was okay to say.

He looked at his watch again, then pulled the truck door shut and hit the ignition in frustration. "I'm late picking up Cole from preschool, actually. Can I check back with you later?"

"Of course."

"Tell Sarah we're thinking of her. And let me know when you find out about the ankle."

"You take care of yourself, too, Jake. Sarah tells me you're doing a great job. We're praying for all of you."

He wasn't doing a great job. He was barely scraping by, with Cole paying the price. But he wasn't going to admit that to anyone, much less Sarah or Dorothy. "Thanks" was all he said as he pulled out of the parking lot faster than he ought to have and barreled toward the preschool.

It was already 11:27. He wasn't going to make it on time. Again.

Chapter Two

Emma tried to hide the fact that she was looking at the clock on the wall. She tried not to feel the sadness that pushed down Cole's shoulders as each of the other children trotted out the door with their mother or father.

Jake was late. Again. He'd been consistently late—and if not late, then often the last—to pick the boy up from school. Children noticed these things. How could she make Jake understand that a child with such an acute sense of abandonment as Cole was prone to it even more?

"He's coming?" Cole's voice held too much worry.

To Cole, this wait wasn't just a few minutes, it was an eternity doubled by the particular sadness of being last. It wasn't fair to judge when Jake was already facing so many struggles, but Emma wished Jake could see the look in his nephew's eyes right now. See the way his tiny shoulders sank as he peered quietly out the window into the empty parking lot.

"I'm sure he's coming. You know your uncle, he's just very busy right now." Jake was unorganized, impulsive and inconsistent, but she could still see how much the man cared about Cole. Jake had a great big heart somewhere under all that swagger. She just had to find a way to help Jake see what Cole needed most right now—dependability, and maybe not to be last so much. *Help me find a way to make him understand this, Lord. It seems small, but it's so important.*

Emma tried to make cheery conversation. "So, how did Oscar and Otto settle in over the weekend?"

"They like it. Uncle Jake gave me green beans to feed 'em and they ate 'em right up."

"Did they now?"

Cole made a face. "Then he gave *me* green beans at dinner and said I had to eat 'em up, too."

Emma tried to hide her surprise that Jake had even cooked a dinner, especially one including green beans. But she gave him points that he'd tried to use the turtles as incentive for Cole to eat his vegetables. Jake did manage to surprise her every once in a while. Oh, he had a long way to go in the childcare department, but for a bachelor newbie, he managed a tiny victory every now and then.

With a spray of gravel, Jake's truck sped into the parking lot. Cole jumped up. "There he is!" The relief in the boy's voice twisted Emma's heart.

Jake ducked out of the truck and sprinted to the school door. "I'm sorry, buddy. Last again."

"It's okay," Cole said softly.

No, it's not, Emma wanted to plead but stayed silent.

Jake looked at Emma. "Do you have a minute?"

"Of course," Emma replied just as Pastor Newton came up behind him. She'd had more than one conversation with the reverend about the challenges Jake was facing with Cole. The whole church was trying to help, but Jake declined many of the offers. Sure, some of the church grandmothers could be seen as more meddling than helpful, but Emma worried Jake's pride was making him miss out on a lot of good and useful support.

"Hey, Pastor, you should probably hear this, too," Jake said as he led Cole to the small parlor just off the pre-school entrance. Emma wondered what could require such a conversation as she and Pastor Newton followed them into the room. Jake took Cole's backpack and sat with Cole on the small couch, the boy's feet and bright red sneakers dangling far off the ground next to Jake's long legs and dusty boots.

"Everything okay, Jake?" Pastor Newton asked as he and Emma took the chairs on either side of the couch.

"I'm late," Jake explained to both of them, "because I was on the phone with a friend of Gam's."

Emma liked that Jake put the situation in Cole's perspective, calling her Gam—the name Cole used for his grandmother—instead of Sarah. It was another of those tiny surprises that fueled a reluctant fondness for the man. And kept her feeling hopeful about Jake's care of Cole. "She fell down this morning and hurt her ankle."

Cole's eyes widened. "Gam's hurt?"

Jake gave a bright, forced-casual half smirk, half grimace. "Not too bad. She hurt her leg, so she can't get around too good. But, hey, it's just for a while. She's going to be just fine." He stuck out one leg and pointed to his foot as he wiggled it around. "I broke my ankle once, too, you know. Works just fine now. Gam's'll be the same, just you watch."

Emma could easily read the message Jake was sending. Sarah had broken her ankle, which was not a simple injury. And while Jake was doing his best to reassure Cole, the look Pastor Newton gave her broadcast the same thing she was thinking: Sarah wouldn't be just fine very soon, and that had big consequences for the people in this room.

"I'm so sorry to hear that," Pastor Newton said.

"So," Jake went on in a tone clearly designed to say *no big deal*, "it looks like it'll just be you and me for a while longer." He was striving to make it sound like this was no trouble at all. She knew better. Still, her heart went out to Jake for trying to make sure Cole didn't feel like he was any kind of burden. Even if the truth was very much the opposite. Well, maybe *burden* was the wrong word, but *giant complication* came close. Maybe now the man would accept some of the help the church stood ready to give him.

"But before Christmas, surely?" she dared to ask.

Jake pulled the baseball cap from his head and ran a hand through his hair. He had a dusty, rough-and-tumble charm despite the stress his gesture revealed. "Hope so."

That was five weeks away. Quick looks flashed between the adults in the room. Emma felt the question clang through her brain: *Can you last a month?*

Pastor Newton sat back in his chair. "Well now, there you go. God still sees around corners, as I always say."

Emma wasn't quite sure what to make of the cryptic remark.

"Huh?" Jake replied, looking as stumped as Emma felt.

The reverend addressed his next remark to Cole. "Your Uncle Jake's been stepping in great to take care of you, hasn't he, Cole?"

"Yes, Pastor," Cole said, smiling up at Jake. "And Oscar and Otto, too."

When the pastor raised an eyebrow, Emma added, "Cole has two new pet turtles."

"Well isn't that grand?" the pastor replied. "I know how much you like turtles, Cole."

"Yep."

"So it's going to be a while before your grandmother gets to come and meet Oscar and Otto, which makes the reason I was coming over here to talk to Miss Emma that much more important."

Emma wasn't aware Pastor Newton had been coming over here to talk to her. Why?

"I just got off the phone with Bo Carter. We were talking about my basement remodeling, but he mentioned you and how he admired the way you were holding up. I can't help but think it's a whopper of a challenge to do the work you do with a little guy like Cole in tow. And now that challenge will be with you for longer than we thought. Seems Norma's idea might be a good one."

Norma Binton's idea? Emma worked to hide her suspicion. Norma Binton was on the preschool board—actually, she thought she *ran* the preschool board, even though she was only vice-chair. Norma made no secret of her desire that her niece be considered the top candidate for the Preschool Director position. It was unkind—but not without reason—to worry that any idea Norma had about Emma would involve improving her niece's chances for the post and lessening Emma's.

Emma wasn't surprised Jake's eyes narrowed a bit. People didn't call Norma Binton "Old Biddy Binton" for no reason. "What idea does…" for a split second Emma worried Jake would use the nickname in front of Cole, but he didn't "… Miss Binton have?"

Pastor Newton leaned forward and steepled his hands.

"Well, to tell the truth, we were already thinking we would need to get Sarah some help. And now we definitely need to do that for you, Jake. After all, a little boy and a pair of turtles can be a handful—in the best way, of course. We've got lots of people offering to do bits and pieces here and there, but that can be hard to manage. A parade of faces, no matter how helpful, can be a bit much."

"I suppose," Jake said. Emma could tell from his expression that he was wondering where this was heading as much as she was.

Pastor Newton shifted his gaze toward Emma. "What would you say if I told you we were prepared to give you whatever support and time you needed to step in and provide childcare for Cole?"

"Me?" Emma was ashamed of how shocked she must have sounded.

"Her?" Jake echoed.

"Cool!" Cole gave his immediate approval of the idea. Emma wondered if Pastor Newton—and maybe even Norma Binton—knew exactly how fast that would happen.

"We could easily arrange it so Miss Emma could watch you when you're not here in school." Before Emma could draw a breath to question the wisdom of the idea, the pastor went on. "Oh, I know it's a challenge, with the projects already on your plate, but we can all pitch in. And you're already so organized."

Emma tried not to be swayed by the sweet look in Cole's eyes. "It would be…complicated."

"It'd be fun," Cole declared. "She already helped us with the turtles and everything."

"We've had loads of folks offering to help with all

that's happened, Jake. Only I think helping out in pre-school is a better place for all those willing volunteers if it keeps Cole's life consistent with people he knows and trusts, like Emma." He leaned toward Cole. "Would you like Miss Emma to help take care of you while your uncle is at work?"

Cole nodded enthusiastically. "Yep!"

Pastor Newton turned to Jake. "You can see your way clear to letting Emma help out, can't you, Jake?"

At first Emma thought Pastor Newton was being in-sensitive, having this conversation in front of Cole. Now she realized he was being entirely too clever. The rever-end knew neither Jake nor Emma would refuse the idea in front of Cole, given his enthusiasm.

She wasn't sure what to make of Jake's slow smile. "I think I can live with that."

"Emma?" Pastor Newton pressed.

How could she refuse now? It didn't matter that she barely had enough time to meet all the demands in front of her. The church's living nativity had been given to her to coordinate. Just because the church library reno-vation project—an expansion of the children's section designed to serve the preschool that had been Natalie Wilson's pet project—was likely on hold didn't mean she could take this on.

Yet one truth trumped them all: this little boy had just lost his mother and father. What kind of person would put a crèche or a library or a director's post before that?

"Of course I'll say yes." She gave Cole the warmest smile she could manage given the knots tangling in her stomach. "I haven't really gotten a chance to get to know Otto and Oscar, after all." At the very least, it would mean she'd be taking Cole home from preschool, so there would be no sitting here waiting while Jake scrambled to arrive.

"Hooray!" Cole shouted. "Do we start today?"

Pastor Newton laughed. "Can you scrape by until Wednesday while we pull some details together?"

Jake's grin looked entirely too much like Cole's. "I think I can live with that."

Jake pulled into the driveway of Cole's home Wednesday afternoon with a sense of calm he hadn't known for weeks. Knowing Emma had Cole finally allowed the frantic rushing to subside—well, at least enough to let him catch a deep breath or two. He liked having Emma around. Her presence made him feel better about getting through this gap until Sarah returned, even if he still didn't quite know how he was going to pull it off. Living here at Nat and Kurt's house he could manage. The logistics were doable—especially with how organized Emma was. But the emotional stuff? Cole's grief, the nightmares, the upcoming holidays that would never be the same? He definitely needed Emma's help with those.

He paused for a moment with his hand on the knob of the house's side door, his own sense of Natalie's loss rushing up to tighten his throat. This grief was like living in a lightning storm—a strike of pain could come out of nowhere to take you down at moments that often made no sense.

This was Nat's home. She was supposed to be here, gearing up for happy family holidays with Kurt and Cole. Jake knew it made sense to stay here, to keep Cole in his own room and his own bed and the place the boy knew best. And when Sarah recovered, she'd be moving in here, so as little as possible would change in Cole's life. For these reasons, Jake gladly made the sacrifice of sleeping—or at least trying to sleep—in Natalie's guest room. The gaping pain of the empty master bedroom down the hall, however, kept him awake most nights.

He pushed the door open to quiet—something he wasn't expecting. And the spectacular scent of something baking. Setting down his gear in the hallway, Jake walked toward the kitchen to find Emma sitting at the table doing paperwork. "Where's Cole?"

"He fell asleep on the couch after we made muffins," Emma said quietly. She had an adorable smudge of flour on one cheek. "I carried him upstairs to his room."

"You got him to take a nap?" Jake asked with sincere admiration. He hadn't been able to accomplish that feat a single time since he'd taken over parenting duties.

"You should wake him up in an hour so he doesn't have trouble falling asleep tonight," she advised as a timer on the oven went off.

"He has a tough time falling asleep every night. And staying asleep when he does. I understand now why sleep deprivation can be used as a form of torture."

Emma laughed softly as she used a set of oven mitts to slide a tray of sumptuous-smelling muffins from the oven. It was a tender, musical laugh. No wonder the kids flocked to her. "Natalie must have let him help a lot— Cole's a lot of fun in the kitchen," she said.

"He didn't get that from me." Jake said it as a joke, but it just seemed to underscore how Natalie would never be cooking in this kitchen again. Another pang of grief-lightning struck as he realized he'd never get another batch of cookies or cinnamon rolls from Nat. "You have no idea how good that smells."

Emma set the tray onto a little metal grate to cool.

"Baking feels peaceful. My dad was in real estate, and he would sometimes heat up a little bit of vanilla in a dish before he showed a house. He said it made it smell like home."

"My dad's idea of home was a case of beer in the fridge." Jake wasn't sure what made him say that, except to acknowledge that he and Nat hadn't grown up in such a postcard-perfect home. "Maybe that's why Nat was so good at this kind of stuff."

"She was a great mother." Emma pulled the mitts from her hands. "That'll stay with Cole, you know. Even though he's young, it's not lost forever."

Jake's throat tightened even more. Emma had a way of saying things that stuck deep in his chest—it was both comforting and excruciating at the same time. "Um, yeah," he muttered as he pulled a can of soda from the fridge. "Actually, I wanted to talk to you about something like that." The idea had come to him this afternoon, lodging so firmly in him that he knew he had to make it happen. He sat down at the table, taking the fact that he'd come here to a quiet house, able to have a conversation, as affirmation to move forward. "I want to do the library thing."

Emma sat down opposite him. "The library thing? The expansion?"

"Nat was talking to me about doing the building, about Car-San donating part of the supplies cost before…" How long would it be before he could finish a sentence like that without his gut twisting up? "Well, you know. I still want to do it. It's what she would have wanted, you know?" The last sentence caught thick and sad in his throat.

"We put the project on hold, given everything," Emma

replied. "Are you sure? You've got a lot on your plate with Cole."

"It's way easier with you here." The admission felt a bit bold, but it was true. It had only been one day and already he felt more in control than he had since the night Kurt and Nat died. Having Emma here changed the whole feel of the house and his day. "And I...well, I think I need to do this. I don't want anyone else to do the work. It needs to be me."

"I can understand that, but does it need to be now?"

"Yeah, it does." Jake hoped he wouldn't have to explain why, because he didn't really know where the urgency came from, only that it would not go away.

Emma looked wary. "It's Zosia's decision, not mine."

"But she'll listen to you," Jake urged. "I gotta do this. Can you make her see that?" It probably wasn't smart. It might be more than he could handle. But the moment he'd come to the realization, "no" simply wasn't an option. Somehow it felt as if his sanity, his ability to keep on for Cole's sake, hung on making that library project happen. Emma was the kind of person who could understand that, wasn't she?

"I mean it—I'll go convince Zosia if I have to." He gave her the most direct and insistent look he dared. "I think I can even find ways to let Cole help. I...we...need to make this happen."

Relief washed over him when she nodded. "I'll talk to Zosia. She has the approval, but she and the board did put me in charge of overseeing the project with Natalie. So now I'll just oversee it with you. And Cole."

She understood. She recognized his crazy need to make Natalie's project happen now that she was no longer here to complete it herself. He may never be able to explain why this was such a foothold for him, but any foothold—even something as nonsensical as this—was a victory right now.

As was the quiet house. "A nap, huh? Wanna tell me how you managed that trick?"

A small smile brightened her face. She had one of those sweet, heart-shaped faces that had always been a weakness of his. Even while she jutted her chin out at him and said, "You may not like the answer."

"The boy is napping. The house is quiet. I already love the answer." The lack of quiet these days frayed his nerves. And if he had trouble keeping up with Cole, how on earth had Sarah managed it?

Emma folded her hands on the table, and he felt a lecture coming on. "Routine and consistency. Children Cole's age thrive on it. And with everything he's been through, he needs it even more." She leveled him with what Jake suspected was her serious teacher face. Oh, she might be all small and slight and soft—he'd not failed to notice all those blond waves and her fair skin and light blue eyes—but she was good at pointed looks. "You're going to have to slow down."

Seriously? It felt like he was trudging through mud already. Everything took so much longer with Cole around. "Slow down? It used to take me seventeen minutes to get out of the house in the morning. Now I'm thrilled if I make it in under an hour."

Another look. She really was good at this. "Which is exactly why I'm worried about you taking on the library. It's probably the last thing you need."

He decided to give her a look of his own. "You're wrong. It's the one thing I need." The sound of Cole padding his way down the stairs drew the conversation to a close. "I'll slow down and do the routine thing as best as I can, but you get me on the library thing. I promise I'll deliver on both. Deal?"

Cole's voice came groggily from the bottom of the stairs. "Hi, Miss Emma. Hi, Uncle Jake."

"Hello, Cole." Emma's voice switched from lecturing teacher to the warm, honeyed tone he suspected drew the kids so strongly to her. "I'll talk to Zosia," she said, and Jake found he didn't mind that sweet tone used on him.

Cole climbed onto Jake's lap, still groggy from sleep. He reached for the soda on the table. "Can I have some?"

When Emma gave Jake another look, he said, "Just a sip." Then he lowered one eyebrow at her over Cole's head in a *give me a break* expression. "Then how about some milk and an apple?"

He'd show Emma Mullins he could get the hang of this.

Chapter Three

Emma had expected the first preschool board meeting after Natalie's death to be difficult, but not quite this challenging. Zosia, as director, usually attended the preschool board meetings the third Thursday of every month. Today she was coming in late, as she'd been in Denver with her husband at a doctor's appointment.

November and December were always challenging months at the school. The crunch of holidays hyped the children up and offered dozens of distractions. Families were busy, traveling and stressed. The trauma of Kurt and Natalie's accident made everything worse. The police had not found the shooter responsible. And no matter how many times they put forth the theory that it had been an isolated, random incident, the unspoken "it could happen again" lurked in the backs of everyone's minds. Parents hugged their children extra tight. Attendance at church services had risen. The canyon was reeling in any number of ways from the trauma—and the children picked up on all of it.

People like Emma—those who had already had the randomness of life take a hard whack at them—responded to such stress in different ways. Emma had learned at a young age how unfair life could be. She already knew how the people you loved could be snatched from you in a heartbeat. Everyone else seemed to reawaken to the fact in the aftermath of such a tragedy.

Emma was glad that the first half of the meeting was devoted to Pastor Newton laying out plans he and Zosia had made to offer extra support and encouragement to stunned young parents. "Overcaution is a natural reaction," Pastor Newton said. "So we'll allow it, but we'll also gently rein it back when necessary."

"In other words," Emma added, "next week's trip to the carousel is still on, but if some of the parents feel they need to come supervise, we'll let them." She welcomed the chance to show her ability to lead the school, even if it was just in a board meeting.

The Wander Canyon carousel was probably just what these kids needed. Emma could think of no better balm than the happy laughter of little boys and girls on the town's beautiful carousel. This one—with all kinds of animals except ponies—was one of the first things she'd fallen in love with about the town when she moved here two years ago. She'd had enough time with this year's class that she could easily predict which of the animals each child would choose. Of course, Cole would claim the turtle, but Emma also knew Heidi would likely favor the ostrich, Luke would go for the eagle, and Brittany would most definitely opt for the flamingo. Knowing Jake had lived in Wander Canyon his whole life, she found herself wondering which animal he would choose. The bold lion, most likely.

"That's a wise approach, Emma," Pauline Walker agreed. A wonderful older woman who'd moved to

Wander Canyon after marrying Hank Walker, one of the prominent local ranchers, Pauline had quickly become one of Emma's favorite members of the church and the school board.

Norma Binton clicked her pen as if Pauline's compliment irritated her. "Where do we stand with the new director candidates?" Emma could have predicted Norma would bring that up. "I see no need to put that aside on account of what's happened."

The carousel had a porcupine, and Emma had often wondered if that had been Norma's favorite animal as a child. She certainly was as prickly.

"Of course not," Pastor Newton said. "As I said at the last meeting, Zosia tells me we have a fine pool of candidates." He directed that last remark to Norma, as if to reassure the woman her niece was most definitely among them. "Zosia expects to make her recommendations at the January meeting."

"That will give us plenty of time to get the new director installed before I leave in February," Zosia said as she entered the room calling her usual *"Dzień dobry"* Polish morning greeting.

"I still don't see why you can't finish out the year," Norma pressed, even as the other board members extended Zosia a greeting and asked about her husband. Emma caught sight of a good bit of eye rolling at Norma's remark, as some form of this conversation had taken place at the last three meetings.

Zosia shucked off her coat. "Well, tell that to Jason's knee. We've pushed off the replacement until after the holidays as it is." She took her place beside Emma. "Really, Norma, it's not as if I'm leaving the country. I'll be able to come back and do a few visits in the spring. And Emma will be here to help guide things along."

Zosia had made it clear that she preferred Emma to shift into the director's position, but Norma had convinced the board to do a full search and foisted her niece into the candidate pool.

"Of course," Norma acknowledged. "Which leads us right into asking about the projects she's heading up."

"Emma and I are set to discuss the nativity cast next week," Pastor Newton offered despite Norma's pointed glare in Emma's direction. "I'd say we're ahead of schedule."

"Are you sure you can take all this on given your new…responsibilities?" another board member asked.

"Do you mean Cole?" Emma replied. "Of course." Despite her own niggling worries that tending to Cole on top of her duties with the crèche and the library would put her organizational skills to the test, she wasn't about to admit to anything short of absolute confidence in front of Norma Binton. "Like Pastor Newton said, we're ahead of schedule on the crèche. But I do have some news regarding the library expansion."

"Are we really going through with that?" Pauline asked. "I mean, it was Natalie's project and all."

"Emma's had a request from Jake Sanders." Zosia announced.

Norma's face pinched into a frown. "Shouldn't that be your role, Zosia?"

"Not if you all have placed Emma in charge of the library," Zosia replied. Zosia shared Emma's suspicion that the double project load was a test of sorts—at least to Norma—and had offered to support Emma in any way she could. "Emma, tell them what Jake has asked."

Emma made sure she met each of the board members' eyes with direct confidence. "Jake wants to move ahead on the construction. Natalie had been talking to him about it before she passed. You know she was planning on asking Car-San to donate materials and hopefully labor."

"Yes, but given what's happened…" another member began.

"Given what's happened, Jake is doubly committed to doing the project. And doing it now. He sees it as a way to honor his sister."

"Pastor, didn't you mention Jake has been late to school with Cole every day since the grandmother left?" Norma seemed to feel compelled to point out.

"And I hear Sarah broke her leg and won't be back for two months!" another member warned.

Pastor Newton held up his hands. "We don't know if it's two months or just a few weeks. Jake just got the news."

"I worry that man has too much on his mind to add the library," Pauline said.

"It's become very important to him," Emma said. "I don't think we should take it away from him just because of Cole and Sarah."

Norma glowered at Zosia. "Do you agree with this? Putting an important church project in the hands of a man already grieving his sister and scrambling to take care of a child?"

"Why?" challenged Pauline. "Are you looking to take it on?"

"Of course not," Norma snapped in reply. "But I question the wisdom of putting Jake and Emma in charge of this, given the circumstances."

"Actually," Pastor Newton said, "I think it's wise to

put them in charge given the circumstances. I don't doubt for a minute that Emma can handle it. And the project represents much more to Jake now. It may be the best place for him to work through his grief."

"Or get lost in it," Norma muttered.

Pauline planted her hands on the table. "That's enough of that, Norma. The young man hasn't given us any reason to think we can't count on him. And it's a library. It's not as if lives are at stake if it's not ready when we want it to be."

That silenced Norma, but didn't squelch the sour look that seemed to be a permanent fixture on the woman's face. From her first days here, Wander Canyon had felt like such a kind town to Emma. It always baffled her how Norma could be raised around so much goodwill and keep such a sour spirit.

"So it's settled, then?" Pastor Newton looked around the room. "Jake Sanders will take on the library expansion project under Emma's supervision. And if I may, I'd like to propose to Jake and Sarah that the memorial funds we received honoring Kurt and Natalie be used to purchase new children's books."

Emma watched Zosia and Pauline look directly at Norma, as if to challenge her to find any fault with the idea. Norma only nodded and kept silent.

"I'll tell Jake about the approval when he drops Cole off tomorrow morning," Emma said as she gathered her things to end the meeting.

Norma raised one gray eyebrow. "On time, I hope?"

Emma sorely wanted to remind Norma that she'd never known the challenges of parenting. And that it was easy to be excruciatingly punctual when you had no one else to worry about. And evidently easy to look down on people from the high judgmental tower Norma had built around herself. If Old Biddy Binton spent as much time among the joyful, noisy, messy, loving children of the preschool as she did sitting around a table debating policies, she might be a different woman.

"Will you look at us?" Jake called to the smiling face in the back seat of his truck cab. "Fifteen whole minutes early!"

Jake allowed himself a moment of victorious pride as he pulled the truck into the preschool parking lot. Among the *first* cars in the parking lot. Not just on time, but *early*. He liked to think Natalie was smiling down on his new parental feat. He had certainly looked forward to—and now thoroughly enjoyed—the smile on Emma's face as she stood in the doorway waving a cheery welcome.

Seeing his teacher's wave, Cole scrambled to unbuckle himself from the booster seat and nearly bolted out of the truck across the parking lot before Jake snagged him by the sleeve of his jacket at the last minute. "Whoa, boy. You can't just fire off into a parking lot like that." He was going to say, "You could get squashed by a car," but caught himself. *I can't say stuff like that in front of Cole.* If he had his way, the boy would never learn the gruesome details of how his parents had died. As it was, Jake felt he would never get the picture of Nat's red minivan crushed into a nearly unrecognizable shape against the overpass pillar out of his mind.

Jake offered Cole a brief smile and squeezed him to his side, brushing off the eerie sensation Pastor Newton had called "a chill to the soul." One of those seemed to come daily, triggered by almost anything, even things that made little sense. He could often see some similar little shudder come over Cole. Unqualified as he might be, he and Cole were in this together, and he was going to make sure they came out of it intact.

"We're early!" Cole cried with a glee that made Jake flinch. Granted, it was a feat, but Cole made it sound as if Jake had parted the Red Sea. He decided to take that as a pint-size compliment rather than a frank assessment of his lack of punctuality.

"You are indeed! Good for you!" Emma said, welcoming Cole with a joyful hug. "You're the first one here."

Cole twisted around to grin at Jake. "First!"

"Well, whaddaya know." Jake enjoyed the feeling of his own grin. Grins were hard to come by these days. Emma's grin? Well, that just made his widen all the more.

"What did the trick?" she asked as they both followed Cole to the set of cubbies where the boy knew to hang his coat and his little turtle backpack.

Jake knew he'd have to own up to it. "Well, it may or may not have something to do with the fact that *someone* laid out Cole's clothes for the next day on his bedroom chair." He'd gone up into Cole's room the previous night to find a set of boy's clothes laid out carefully. Cole had taken a rather uncle-humbling pride in showing Jake the purpose of the setup and how it would help them get ready in the morning. To be late after an intervention like that would have been humiliating, hence today's extra-punctual arrival.

"I thought that might help," Emma said. Did he imagine her wink? The way her eyes lit up tingled at the back of Jake's neck. It made him want to be on time every school morning from here on out.

She motioned for Cole to head on into the classroom, where Zosia was waiting with an equally wide smile at his prompt arrival. "*Dzień dobry*, Mr. First One Here. Go ahead and pick your task for the day."

Cole gave Jake another triumphant grin. "That means good morning. First one here gets to pick."

Jake leaned in toward Emma as Cole took off in the direction of a giant board picturing different tasks with little squares of children's photos lined up beside them. "I didn't know there were bribes involved."

Emma crossed her arms playfully over her chest as they both watched Cole go straight to Feed Zippy and plunk his picture down on that spot. "I prefer to think of them as incentives."

When was the last time he had felt the simple pleasure of innocent teasing? Jake offered her a sideways glance at the shiny term. She laughed and relented. "Well, prizes, maybe. After all, it's much better to reward the good behavior than to punish the bad."

It was such a teacher thing to say. But Jake didn't mind. He gave himself a moment to bask in the glow of Emma's favor. This was much better than the shade of her chiding, gentle as it was. She was fun to please, and he didn't quite know what to do with how much he liked it.

As they started to walk back toward the entrance, Emma stopped him. "Don't forget to say goodbye to Cole."

He didn't have to ask if that was important. In fact, he wanted to kick himself for getting distracted by Emma's approval. This was definitely not the time to let his brain get waylaid by her heart-shaped face or the memorable pink of her cheeks. Now had to be all about Cole.

Jake ducked his head back into the room and called, "See you at dinner, buddy. It's burger night."

Cole threw his hands up in a half wave, half cheer.

"Hooray! Bye, Uncle Jake." Cole looked happy. Not rushed or worried or even sad. That was a gift of a way to start any day. He ought to thank Emma, but he couldn't think of a way to do it that didn't sound too, well, personal.

"I've got a bit of a prize for you, too," Emma said as he reached the door. "You're good to go on the library project."

Her relief surprised him. "Was there a doubt?" Who on earth would deny him the chance to honor his sister with the project she'd been working on? It wasn't as if Wander Canyon was overrun with construction companies willing to donate the materials like Car-San was. Truth be told, he was a tiny bit peeved she felt she even had to get approval for him to do it.

"When Norma Binton is on the committee, I never take anything for granted."

He'd been surprised when Old Biddy Binton had come calling with a casserole for him just after he'd taken up parenting duty. She'd taken three to Sarah already. His surprise turned to annoyance when he realized she'd included a stack of a parenting magazines with the dish. The only source of parenting advice he currently wanted to heed was standing in front of him. "Norma. Don't I hear you on that one."

As a stream of cars began to pull into the parking lot, Jake liked to think the other moms and dads were pleasantly surprised to see his pickup already there. "I should be home about four thirty," he advised Emma. An appealing thought struck him. "Speaking of prizes, maybe you'd like to join us for burger night? I'm a master at the grill. Hoards clamor for my secret recipe." It would be nice to celebrate the thrill of finally doing something right—and to have some dinner conversation at a higher-than-preschool level.

"Dinner?"

Her hesitation and startled eyes stung a bit. Evidently he had imagined the wink. "Well, yeah. Seems silly for you to leave, and it's the least we can do for incentivizing our timely arrival. Besides, I don't think I can choke down another casserole." His burgers definitely beat out any casserole in the state, but this was more about company than cuisine.

She tucked her hair behind one ear as she shifted her gaze out to the parents in the parking lot. "Oh, I don't know if that's such a good idea."

She was worried what people might think. He supposed she had to be, given her position. The phrase they used to bat around as teenagers—"Wander's always watching"—was still true. It bugged him anyway. He liked the idea of having dinner with her. He wanted to thank her. How was his offer any different from the dozen meals folks had foisted on him in the past days? "It's just a burger, Emma. Well, no burger I make is *just* a burger, but you know what I mean." The joke fell short.

She blushed, and Jake's irritation at all the Norma Bintons in the world who would deny him the pleasure of a decent burger with a pretty girl churned in his chest. "I'd better not."

Whether Wander was watching or not, Jake never gave five minutes' notice to how people regarded him. He simply didn't care. Was he going to have to start caring now? Or just watch in annoyance at how much Emma had to? He couldn't remember the last time a woman had turned down a dinner invitation from him. The fact that it came from *her* just made it worse.

"Hey, no big deal. It was just a thought. See you around four thirty." He tried to walk casually toward his truck. Emma's expression told him he hadn't been successful in his attempt to brush it off as no big deal. If she felt she had to watch herself, he had no right to argue with her caution.

But he didn't have to like it.

Chapter Four

Emma sat on the couch that afternoon, paging through a pile of Christmas-story picture books with Cole. The boy was holding a stack of sticky notes, and she let him flag a page that had something she wanted to incorporate into the church's living crèche.

"So these are all the animals that were in the stable with Baby Jesus on the night He was born," she explained as they turned to a particularly beautiful page. "See the donkeys and the horses and the cows?" Just for fun she softly sang "the cattle are lowing, the poor baby wakes" from "Away in a Manger." Not wanting to risk the chaos of real animals despite the ready supply from local ranches, Emma had decided on life-size cutouts to augment the human cast. This page had a particularly beautiful arrangement, so she pointed to the sticky notes in Cole's hands. "Let's mark this page."

Cole dutifully pasted a note on the top of the page. "Were there turtles?"

She'd been waiting for that question. "Well, nobody knows for sure, but maybe not. Turtles like it where it's wet, and this was a desert kind of place." When a frown crossed the boy's face, she added, "But you never know. God created all the animals, so maybe lots of them traveled far to see Him."

"Like the wise guys," Cole said.

It took Emma a minute to catch his meaning. "You mean the Wise Men who came to see Jesus?" It didn't take much imagination to figure out where Cole's unusual term for the Magi might have come from. Jake's quick, if offbeat, sense of humor was one of his better qualities. He'd lost a lot of it lately, and she liked the idea that her help was giving it back to him bit by bit.

"Uncle Jake and I were talking about the stable scene last night. He says you're running it, and that you'd have to find a Joseph and a Mary and a Baby Jesus, and some wise guys."

Emma laughed, even if she did take issue with Jake's irreverent title. "He's right."

"Who's gonna be Baby Jesus? I'm too big for that."

She heard Jake come through the door as she agreed, "You certainly are." But was there some role he could play? A little drummer boy, perhaps? She'd have to ask Pastor Newton what he thought of adding the character to the crèche. While she wasn't sure it was strictly biblical, Cole certainly deserved a special experience like that.

"You certainly are what?" Jake asked as he came into the room.

"I'm too big to be Baby Jesus in the stable," Cole said, sliding off the couch to give his uncle an endearing hug.

Emma liked that Jake crouched down to hug Cole at his level. She'd always found the practice of getting down eye to eye with young children a trait of good parenting. She wondered if the position was a natural instinct on Jake's part or coaching from his sister. Natalie had been an outstanding, attentive mother. The signs of it were all over this house. It gave Emma pangs of sorrow to see the rich family life Cole enjoyed displayed in the homey touches of this place. She could only imagine what it was doing to Jake to live here. It impressed her that he'd made that sacrifice to give Cole every shred of normalcy possible. When Jake Sanders settled down—which certainly wouldn't be anytime soon—he'd make a very good husband and father to the right woman.

"Oh, you're definitely too big to do the Baby Jesus gig," Jake said. "I think you grew a whole inch last week. By Christmas you may be big enough to be Joseph's cool brother."

"I must have missed that verse in the stories," Emma joked.

"I *told you* there's no brother in the story," Cole said, giggling.

"There oughta be. Or a cool uncle. Everyone should have one of those."

"We were just discussing the wise guys," Emma offered, piling the stack of books into a bag. She'd begun to be just the tiniest bit sorry to leave this house and return to the quiet of her own place. "You must have a very inventive nativity scene at your house."

"I don't do much holiday decorating. But if I had a nativity scene, I think it would have a cool brother." He turned his gleaming smile toward Cole with a wink. "And most definitely a turtle."

"Told ya!" Cole said as he looked back at Emma. "How long till burgers, Uncle Jake? I'm hungry."

Jake straightened up. "Suddenly I'm eating dinner at Florida early bird special hours. Don't let that get out or I may never live it down."

Cole walked up to Emma. "You wanna stay for burger night?"

Emma looked at Jake, who shrugged a silent "I didn't put him up to it." Emma wasn't quite sure she believed him. "Oh, I don't know, Cole." She couldn't bring herself to say an outright no to those wide eyes. Jake's eyes were definitely inviting her to stay, as well.

"Whatcha got for dinner at your house?" Cole asked.

Now that was a trick question. As a single woman living alone, dinner often was yogurt or a bowl of soup or even cereal. She'd never mastered the art of good meals for one. "Not much," she answered, not wanting to admit to the poor choices lurking in her own kitchen.

"We got a million pots of food. Want one of ours?" The child was sweetly offering to share their supply of casseroles. "Some of 'em smell funny." Maybe not so sweet after all.

"There's one in there I can't identify a single thing in. I left mystery meat behind in the high school cafeteria line, thank you very much." Jake pointed to the bag from the local butcher she hadn't realized he'd placed on the counter on his way in. "Burger night is a touch of self-defense."

Emma laughed again. "Your secret is safe with me."

"So stay and eat with us," Cole insisted. "Otto and Oscar want you to, too."

It was touching how the boy went out of his way to tell her how much his turtles appreciated her visits. Perhaps it was his way of safely expressing his need for the attention she could give him. How could she refuse now?

"Well, maybe just to test if your uncle's burgers really are as good as he says they are. But then I have to go."

Jake's gray eyes glinted above a victorious grin.

"Okay, buddy, go upstairs and wash those hands while I get things out. We'll show Miss Emma how it's done." When Cole scrambled up the stairs, he said, "I didn't put him up to it. Honest."

Rather than dispute him, Emma simply chose to offer him a dubious look as she washed her own hands in the kitchen sink. She chose a safer subject. "Wise guys, huh?"

"*Wandering Magi* always sounded a bit stuffy to me." Jake pulled what looked like several pounds of ground beef wrapped in butcher paper out of the bag. That was way more than one man and one boy could eat—which meant he'd planned on the possibility of convincing her to stay. His persistence was as flattering as it was unnerving. The man's personality wasn't what she'd call arrogant, but it certainly was confident.

"And you wonder why nobody ever puts me in charge of things like that," he joked. "We'd end up with a nativity scene that included all the animals on the carousel."

She took a chance. "But could you help me design the stable frame? Last year's got knocked over and broken so I need to build a new one."

"Piece of cake," Jake said. "Now where does someone like Natalie keep her spices?"

"I found the cinnamon in that cabinet next to the stove," Emma offered. "We had cinnamon toast for a snack this afternoon."

"Who doesn't like cinnamon toast?" Jake asked as he sorted through the jars in the cabinet, selecting four of them. "But you have to…"

"Cut it in diagonal triangles, I know," she finished for him. "Cole was very specific."

Jake laughed. "It's a Sanders thing. One of the very

few traditions we managed to carve out of the joke of a family life we had as kids." The shade of bitterness to his words pricked Emma's heart. Clearly, Natalie's enthusiasm for parenting was born out of the happiness she'd lacked as a child. She could understand that. Her own passion for childhood education had taken root in the same barren soil.

Emma settled herself on the counter chair as Jake began adding whatever ingredients made his burgers so awesome. He went about like a man who knew how to feed himself well. Most of the men she knew steered clear of the kitchen. Yet another way Jake didn't fall into the category of *most men*.

"So what about you?" he asked as he worked. "Picture-perfect holidays in your childhood?"

Jake had no idea what he was asking. Emma tried to shrug the question off casually, but his expression told her she hadn't succeeded. "Whoa, wrong question," he stated, one hand on his chest in apology.

The usual sidestepping comments wouldn't suffice. Not for this man and the grief he was still deeply feeling. Maybe it would be okay to talk to him about it, just a little. None of the grisly details, the ongoing strife, but she found she wanted to share just the broad strokes of it with him. "I didn't grow up happy. Well, for most of my childhood. I have some lovely memories of the early years." She paused a bit, feeling like she was dropping a boulder into the room as she said, "Before my mother died."

She watched the words hit him. It was better that he knew. She wasn't ready for everyone to know, but he was okay. He deserved to know.

Jake stilled. "How old were you?" She could see him

bracing himself for her to say that she was the same age Cole had been.

As if any count of years could soften a blow like that. Or the catastrophic damage it left behind. Maybe she could just talk about Mom and leave the tragedies of Dad and Sam out of it. "Ten." She felt like she had to add, "So, older than Cole."

The dashing glint that had been in Jake's eyes melted into pain. "Did it wreck you?" After a second, he seemed to shake out of it and say, "I'm sorry, I didn't mean that the way it sounded. I'm…" He cast his gaze to the stairway Cole had just scampered up. "I'm just so scared he'll never get over this. That it'll ruin him forever."

Jake's grieving heart showed so openly in those final words. Emma thought of the wreck her big brother had become. Losing Mom had indeed ruined Sam forever. The tirades, the disappearing for days, the fights between Dad and Sam—back when they were still talking to each other. In many ways, she and Sam lost both parents when Mom died. Of course, none of that was what Jake needed to hear right now. "It changes you forever," she replied, picking her words carefully. "But it doesn't have to ruin you. Cole has you, and that's going to make a world of difference."

"Who did you have? I mean, you don't seem… wrecked."

Some wrecks you can't see, she wanted to say. Would the truth be too painful for him to hear? Dad had never found his way back out of the grief, instead becoming a hollow and distant man who only looked like her father. And Sam? He was lost in every sense of the word.

The look in Jake's eyes drove Emma to open up. No one else in Wander knew her story. "No one, actually.

At least, not at first. I like to think it was God who kept me safe until an eighth grade teacher reached out." She couldn't help but hold Jake's gaze, despite how raw the words felt. "But that's the thing. It only takes one person who cares. And Cole's already got that in you."

Sam hadn't had that. Hard as she'd tried, she had been just a confused grieving child beside Sam, unable to be that one person, the anchor he needed. What would Sam have become if he'd had a Jake in his life? The question pierced her like a blade. And it begged the question that kept her up too many nights: Could Sam still be saved?

Emma's heart burned to give this desperate man any assurance she could. "Cole's going to be okay."

Jake made a helpless gesture. "Thanksgiving, Christmas…how can it be anything but terrible? How did you manage those first holidays?"

She'd have to tell him a bit more—and Emma couldn't decide if that was better or worse. Still, she felt as if she could trust him. "I remember the last Thanksgiving we had with Mom. It was sweet in all the ways that you don't realize when something is the last time." The recollections felt as if they'd been pulled up from some dark, dusty place, and letting them out into the light didn't hurt as much as she'd expected. "You never know it's the last, do you?"

"No." He said it softly.

"That first Christmas was a blur. I don't even really remember Christmas happening that year." Emma dared to give him the one detail that might sting. "She died on December tenth." It probably would have been safe to tell him that a drunk driver had sent Mom's car careening over an embankment, but she couldn't make herself take that extra step.

"How am I going to pull this off?" It was as vulnerable as she'd ever seen him. Tenderhearted, even, although she knew he'd dislike that word. She was seeing the total opposite of the Jake Sanders most people knew.

She would have liked it if her smile were stronger. But she was proud of herself for even managing to smile at all. "One awesome burger at a time, I suppose." Emma fidgeted as a jolt of exposed panic ran through her, and she quickly added, "Nobody knows that, by the way. The bit about my mother." *And so much more than that.* "So I'd appreciate it if you didn't mention it."

"Sure." He looked puzzled, but offered no more than that.

Jake tried to make hamburgers as if this were an ordinary day. He didn't get to have ordinary days anymore, just days he survived better than others. Today had felt the most ordinary of any day since Natalie died, and it felt like a welcome win when he—or was it Cole?—managed to convince Emma to stay for dinner.

Her admission, however, had just yanked the whole day back into the storm. His entire world had exploded apart the day Nat died. Seemed like every time he got a couple of pieces to fit back together, something would always come apart and demolish the progress.

So Emma's mother had died on December tenth—two weeks before Christmas. It scared him how clear it was that the experience shook her still, all these years later. And how could it not? He knew she was trying to tell him that she'd turned out okay. She was more than okay; in fact, he was coming to really like her. She had a gentle way with all the kids, and yet he'd seen a spunk in her that went beyond preschool-teacher sweetness. He was starting to see her as an alluring woman who'd battled life's blows and still came away with enough joy to share.

None of that stopped the fear of getting it wrong for Cole that continually nipped at Jake's heels. Emma might be okay, but how on earth could Cole ever be? He was only five. He'd lost both parents. Who was Jake kidding that awesome burgers—or any other thing an uncle could do—could save Cole from the monster of sorrow ready to eat him alive? Thanksgiving and Christmas—holidays drenched in family—loomed just around the corner. Jake felt as if he couldn't reach okay himself, much less guide Cole on the way.

"I'm sorry for your loss," he pushed out as he tried to make his hands do the ordinary task of forming hamburger patties, then winced. He'd have slapped his hand over his mouth if his hands weren't currently in the meat. "Man, I promised myself I'd never say that to anyone ever again." And yet he'd said it. To her of all people.

She gave a small sigh. "It does get old, doesn't it?" Was that a smile? A real one, not the fake one she'd forced up a minute ago.

"Or that line about God not sending you more than you can handle. Let's just say the next person who gives me that one may not get the benefit of my better nature."

"They mean well."

Jake pressed a patty onto the platter. "Norma Binton doesn't know how to mean well. She only knows how to be mean." After a second, the oddest thought hit him. "What do you suppose wrecked her?"

"Huh?"

"Well, I've always just thought of Old Biddy Binton as born mean. But I snapped at the cashier in the hardware store today in a way that would have done Norma proud."

Her eyes took on a softness he could have seen from a hundred yards out. A tender kind of glow that reached into all his darkness. "You're not wrecked," she said with a gentle certainty. "And you're not Norma."

Given the amount of anger he was carrying around these days, he wasn't so sure.

Emma leaned one elbow on the counter, relaxing a little bit more from the careful posture she'd held. "The angry stuff is just part of the process, you know."

"Oh, Pastor Newton gave me a little booklet on that whole seven stages of grief thing." He took on a voice like a sports announcer. "Well, folks, that was a fine hit by anger, clean out of the park. Next at bat, we've got bargaining, with depression on deck..." He shook his head, not finding his own joke funny at all. It was hard to find anything funny lately.

He waited for her to say something about his off-key sense of humor, but she didn't. "I've never found it goes in a straight line like that. And people like Norma? They're just trying to be nice and they don't know what to say, so they default to the greeting card lines."

"Or scriptures. Or really bad poems."

She gave him another teacher look. "Or turtles?"

Jake straightened. "Hey, I happen to consider turtles a pretty awesome coping mechanism. Don't knock one of my better moments as an uncle." After a moment, he amended, "Although, two was a better choice than twelve." It took him a second to realize the foreign feeling on his face was a smile. How did she do that to him?

"It made Cole very happy. And that's worth a lot." She paused, then added, "He *can* be happy. Even now. Just in small pieces, but those small pieces are what will get him through."

Jake placed the last patty on the platter. "Thanks."

"For what?"

He dared to come out and say it. "You're the only person who makes me feel like I won't completely mess this up."

That seemed to surprise her. "Really?"

"Lots of people are helping me, but there's this undercurrent of *because you really need it* when they do. It drives me nuts." He picked up the platter and cocked his head toward the door off the kitchen that led to the deck.

"Is that why you strut around like you don't need anyone's help?"

Jake was taking a breath to call her out on that remark when a loud crash came from upstairs and sent them both running.

Chapter Five

Emma watched Jake fighting not to be frantic as he held the ice pack the urgent care nurse had given him to Cole's hairline. "What if he needs stitches?"

She heard Cole's whimper and silently implored Jake to shush that kind of talk. She infused her voice with calm. "Oh, I don't think the cut is that big." When Jake nodded toward the blood on his and Cole's shirts as if that was evidence to the contrary, she reminded him, "Head wounds always bleed way more. A few butterfly bandages and I think he'll be just fine."

The odd term made Cole peek out from under the ice pack. "B-b-butterfly?" His tone was still wobbly and wet, barely above a cry. Poor little guy. He was going to have a sizable bump and most likely a black eye from the tumble he'd taken using a stool to try to get a book off his bookshelf.

"It's a special kind of bandage," she told Cole. "Just for a bump on the head like you got."

"Mark of a tough guy," Jake tried to joke, but too much fear and guilt filled the man's voice. It was touching. Jake may show the world a "walk it off" athlete's demeanor, but he wasn't that man underneath. He'd reacted with so much concern and care when they raced up the stairs to find Cole crying and bleeding in his bedroom.

You should have known better than to leave Cole on his own upstairs like that, Emma chided herself. *You got pulled into that conversation with Jake and forgot why you were there.* Not that she would say any such thing aloud right now. Jake was beating himself up as it was. She'd just have to tell herself to be more careful from here on out, to remind herself why this was one of dozens of reasons to steer clear of Jake's charm and persuasion.

Then again, she was glad she'd been there to calm Jake's panic and help him get the boy to the urgent care center. "I don't know what I'd have done if you weren't there," he said for the tenth time.

"You'd have done this," she reminded him again. "It just would have been a bit harder on your own." More than one of the single parents in her class had told stories of how such emergencies were so much harder to handle without a partner.

"When's it gonna stop hurting?" Cole moaned.

"Soon enough, kiddo," Jake said.

Emma's heart cinched as she watched Jake plant a small kiss on the top of Cole's head. *Thank You, Lord,* she prayed, not for the first time that week, *that Cole has Jake.* She'd meant what she told Jake earlier about it taking only one person who cares to help a child handle a trauma. Jake cared. Way more than she'd expected him to. Had anyone else in Wander seen this side of Jake Sanders? Everyone was well aware of the swagger, the charm, the quick remarks, but she'd been drawn in by the sad and tender heart underneath.

Sam and Dad's hearts had turned hard and brittle after

Mom's death, shattering rather than healing. It was wonderful to see a man who looked as if he'd come out of this without being—what was his term? Wrecked?

An unfamiliar young doctor walked up to them, chart in hand. "Are you Cole's parents?"

"No," Emma and Jake both replied immediately. The question stung at a time like this.

"Uncle," Jake choked out.

"Friend of the family," Emma managed, but that sounded silly.

A nearby nurse Emma recognized rushed up, tapped the young doctor on the shoulder and whispered in his ear. Jake and Emma exchanged glances, well aware of the sad update being relayed.

The doctor looked mortified. "I'm so sorry. I wasn't aware." He changed his tone, squatting down to Cole's level. "I heard you took a tumble, little fella. Can we head on back and take a look?" He glanced up at Emma and Jake. "You can both come in, of course."

Suddenly that felt like too much. "No," Emma said. "Jake is family."

Jake shot her a panicked look. "You'll be fine," she assured him. "I'll be right here if you need me, but you two go on in and take care of things while I wait out here." Cole peeked out from under the ice pack again. "You'll be just fine, Cole. Your Uncle Jake has everything under control."

"Sure looks that way to me," the young doctor said.

Emma was grateful her cell phone went off just then, giving her an easy exit. "I've got to take this anyway," she said, waving Jake and Cole off with the physician.

Her heart fell to her feet when she saw Margaret Washington's name on the screen. The living nativity. She was supposed to present her plans to the worship committee ten minutes ago. Emma squinted her eyes shut as she accepted the call and held the phone to her ear.

"Emma, where are you?"

"I know I'm supposed to be there, Margaret. There was an emergency. With Cole Wilson."

"Good heavens, is Cole okay?" Emma could hear startled questions addressed to Margaret on the other end of the line.

"He took a fall in his bedroom. Knocked his head against the corner of his bookcase. I'm here with Jake at the urgent care center to get it checked out." As the words left her mouth, she realized she'd just informed the entire worship committee that she'd been with Jake and Cole well after "business hours."

The pause at the other end of the line confirmed that realization. "I see," came Margaret's loaded response. "And is the boy all right?"

"Jake is in with Cole and the doctor right now. There was a lot of bleeding, but the cut seems small enough." She felt compelled to add, "Jake was very concerned and wanted to be sure Cole didn't need stitches."

"Poor child. Did Jake not know what to do?"

Emma couldn't say for certain, but the question's implication sounded far more like "Why are you still there with him?" than the words Margaret used.

She worded her answer carefully. "I expect in Jake's line of work this kind of injury is common. It was more about Cole being scared and upset than any lack of first aid skill. He's a fragile little boy right now." Again, the look in Jake's eyes returned to Emma's mind. That man was fragile right now, too—in more ways than he was willing to admit. Trouble was, his inner wounds were starting to call to her just as strongly as Cole's. She'd had to swallow the urge to go into that ER bay with Jake. She should just drop them off at home when all this was over, but she knew she wouldn't.

As if to drive the point home, Margaret asked, "So I take it you won't make this meeting." She didn't sound pleased.

"I'm afraid I won't." *If you'd seen that little boy all bloodied and crying, could you have made it to this meeting, Margaret?* Emma wanted to snap into the phone. Why was the world so good at making it hard to be kind? Especially when it mattered the most? "But if you like, I've got a few minutes now. Why don't you put me on speakerphone and I'll give the committee a rundown of where we are on things?" She'd hoped to impress the committee tonight with her organization, but things clearly hadn't turned out that way.

"I suppose that will have to do."

Emma tucked her cell phone between her shoulder and her ear and rummaged through her bag for her notes. She gave as confident an update as she could manage on costumes and casting and schedules and publicity. She hated that she paused a moment before telling the committee about Jake's willingness to design and build the new stable. It was silly to think anyone would read something into that generosity. Yet this was exactly what she feared: everyone reading things into her interactions with Jake—things that weren't there.

Only there *was* something there. Jake smiled so rarely, but when he did, the power of it lodged in her memory. His charm seemed to be all the more compelling purely because it was so often diluted by sorrow. The man's swagger, which had never appealed to her, fell away to reveal a great big heart broken by loss and worry. He was an extraordinary man, struggling to do his best in an unthinkable situation. She'd be lying if she said that didn't call to her on a deep level. And that was a problem. *Keep me wise, Lord*, she prayed. *So much could go wrong here.*

"So we're pretty much on schedule," Emma concluded, forcing a calm control into her voice despite all the thoughts whirling around in her head.

She would have liked to hear compliments from the committee, but their quiet consent would have to do.

"Surely you will be at school Monday?" Margaret's question had an edge to it, as if this were a test. The preschool met on Mondays, Wednesdays and Fridays—they should know she'd be fine keeping that schedule despite this incident.

Would Jake know what to do if the doctor opted for stitches or warned of a concussion? Knowing Jake, if Cole was still under the weather Monday, he'd bring in a lawn chair and tuck Cole in a corner of his office at Car-San.

And that would have to be okay. Jake was going to need to learn that taking care of a child often meant schedules fell prey to illness or injury. She was already helping way more than she ought to. Jake could manage the weekend without her meddling.

"Of course I will. If Cole won't, I'll make sure Jake is ready to stay home and take care of him during school hours."

That seemed to be the answer Margaret was looking for. "Good." She added, "Tell Cole we'll say a prayer for his recovery."

Make that a prayer for all of us, Emma wanted to add. *We've all got healing to do.*

* * *

Jake was exhausted, hungry and out of his depth. Cole coping with his losses was hard enough. Cole sore, scared, whiny and tired was beyond any uncle skill set he possessed.

He'd almost begged Emma to stay. Which was silly—he was a grown man and Emma had already done far more than anyone had asked her to do.

But this felt so hard. Cole would have a nightmare tonight for sure, and Jake was scraping by on so little sleep as it was. His heart would still race as his mind kept bringing up the vision of Cole's bloody head and frightened eyes. The pile-on of trauma was starting to wear Jake out.

It could have been worse, he told himself. Cole was fine, physically. No stitches, no concussion. A trio of butterfly bandages peeked out from the boy's cowlick of sandy brown hair. Nat had always said it was Kurt's unruly cowlick that first caught her eye. It seemed unfair that tonight's injury struck at Cole's most striking resemblance to his late father. Jake didn't want Cole to feel like the world was out to hurt him, but how do you shield a five-year-old from all this bad stuff?

You shouldn't have left him alone upstairs so long. Nat would have known not to. Nat would never have allowed her attention to be diverted by Emma's eyes or her sweet, soft smile or the way she truly understood his feelings. The sense that he'd failed Cole pressed down on him even more than the fatigue—and that was saying something.

It was late. Cole needed to go to bed but was putting up a monster of a fight. The fifteen minutes Cole had conked out in Emma's car on the way back from the urgent care center seemed to reenergize him. Either that, or it had been the unspoken "what else will go wrong" that widened his nephew's eyes behind the shiner blooming over his right eye.

Nat would know what to do. Emma would know what to do.

But Uncle Jake? He was making this up as he went along. He could rewire a centuries-old house, but putting a preschool boy to bed was the sort of thing so far out of his wheelhouse that the simple task stumped him. As he watched Cole squirm and whine, Jake knew life would never be simple for Cole—or at least, not for a long time. *Passable* or even *not awful* were the best they could hope for. Every single Thanksgiving and Christmas to come without Nat and Kurt? The whole thing was wrong beyond reckoning.

And yet, no amount of such dark thinking changed the fact that Cole needed to sleep, and that meant needing to be tucked in. Giving himself a little internal pep talk, Jake offered what he hoped was a comforting smile and pulled the covers up to his nephew's chin. He ruffled the little guy's hair, careful to steer clear of the cowlick and the bandages. "You're getting an impressive shiner, kiddo."

"Am I? Is that good?" Cole looked so much like his mom in that moment it felt like a shovel was hollowing out Jake's chest.

"Depends on who you talk to." Jake could just imagine the childcare lectures coming his way from Sarah once she heard what had happened. He didn't want to tell her because she'd worry, but she'd skin him alive for keeping it from her.

"What would Mom say?"

How to answer that? "Your guess is as good as mine,"

was the best his taxed brain could come up with at the moment.

For a small stretch of time, Cole fell silent, and Jake said a desperate prayer that the little guy was finally nodding off, until…

"Are Mom and Dad coming back ever?"

The shovel hollowing out Jake's chest turned into a bulldozer. If the Bible talked about wordless prayers of desperation, they surely must have felt like whatever Jake silently shouted toward Heaven at this moment.

He wiped his hands down his face, lost for the right words. "They're…um…well, no. They're not, buddy." A lump the size of the Grand Canyon rose in Jake's throat. "I know that's tough—really tough—but we're gonna get through it. I promise you that."

Cole's eyes started to well up. "Pastor said they're in Heaven. Can't they come back?"

"That'd be really great, wouldn't it?" Jake asked, fighting to keep his composure. It was stretched paper thin, but he had to, for Cole's sake. "But I don't think it works that way." Jake swallowed hard. "You and I, well, we gotta stick it out down here."

Cole gave no answer, but his little arms wrapped more tightly around his stuffed turtle.

"And we got lots of help. We've got Oliver here," Jake tried to sound even the tiniest bit hopeful as he gave the stuffed animal a falsely happy squeeze. "He'll help."

"And Miss Emma," Cole added.

Thank God for Miss Emma, Jake added silently. Tonight it felt like Emma was the only thing holding him upright. Bo was being a great friend and a ridiculously patient partner, but Emma understood this like no one else. "Miss Emma is awesome." She was a lot more than awesome to him lately. She was showing up in his thoughts constantly. For a guy who used to stay out late, it was weird to actually look forward to coming home to Emma and Cole. Was that desperation? Or was there a true attraction growing there?

Jake pulled himself from that line of thought and pointed up to the little tank with its soft yellow light and pair of red-eared slider turtles. "And we got Otto and Oscar, too, now, don't we?" Not everyone agreed with his pet turtle grief-coping strategy—Sarah had audibly gasped when Cole recounted their pet store adventure to his grandmother. But to Jake, it actually felt like one of the few things he'd gotten right in this whole mess. Emma got that. Emma got lots of things.

"And don't forget Gam," he reminded his nephew. "She's a terrific grandma." Sarah would do right by Cole. Even in her own terrible grief—how does anyone bury their child?—she'd stepped right in for her grandson. He and Sarah hadn't seen eye to eye on most things before this, but they'd closed ranks. The past weeks had taught him to count his blessings, and Gam had certainly been one of them.

"Are you gonna be with me now?" The fact that Cole didn't say "gonna be my dad" brought both relief and a stab of pain. No one replaced your dad. Even a bad one. Some people came close, and that was another blessing, but dads were a one-shot deal. You got what you got. Or, in this case, what you lost.

Jake grasped for something useful to say. "I'm here now, but later on when her leg heals Gam's gonna move here to live with you. She and Gamp taught your dad how to ride a bike and all sorts of things."

"I know." Cole did not sound convinced, but at least he yawned.

"You've got a whole bunch of people who love you very much. That hasn't changed. And I'm here." He nearly choked up on the words. Jake had stood up in church five years ago and made a godfather's vow to be there for Cole, and he would. He just never, ever in a million years thought he'd have to make good on that vow like this.

Lost for what else to do, Jake climbed onto the bed, his long legs reaching beyond the pint-size footboard. "How about I sit here with you for a while? Until you fall asleep? We gotta get some shut-eye, you and I. It's been a wild day."

"Yep," Cole said, snuggling up against Jake in a way that made his heart twist in half. "But I'm not sleepy." Cole was yawning as he said that. If he'd had an ounce more energy, Jake might have found that funny.

He made a show of yawning himself—not very hard to fake under the circumstances. "You want me to read a book or something?"

"Nope. I'm okay."

Cole couldn't possibly be okay. Jake wasn't anything close to okay, and he was supposed to be the grown-up here.

Cole yawned again. "Miss Emma said I can't go out and play tomorrow 'cuz of my head."

"I know. You need to rest. But we'll watch a bunch of cartoons or something."

"We never ate our hamburgers."

He didn't want to ask if Cole was hungry. But if a full stomach lulled people to sleep, did an empty one keep them awake? His stomach had been growling for hours, and yet Jake felt as if he could fall asleep on the drive-way. But he did the responsible thing and asked anyway.

"No. But I'm gonna want popcorn tomorrow. We made some at school. Miss Emma knows how to make it *in a pot*."

Jake managed something close to a laugh. "No kid-ding." He only knew how to make popcorn in a micro-wave. Did he need to suffer the humiliation of asking Emma for the recipe? *Was* there a recipe for that? "How about you try closing your eyes for a second."

Cole did. *Please, Lord*, Jake prayed, *have mercy. Let the kid go to sleep.*

"You're gonna stay till Gam comes back, right?"

"Absolutely." It was gut-wrenching how many times a day Cole asked him that. Jake remembered some psy-chological term in the grief booklet Pastor Newton had given him—abandonment issues—and thought again about Cole's chances of "being wrecked."

"Can I keep my sandbox?"

"Nobody's taking anything from here. This is still your house, buddy." He figured he ought to ask, "Got any other questions?"

Cole swiveled his face up to look at Jake. "Did you let me get a turtle because Mom wouldn't?"

Busted. By a five-year-old. How Emma would have grinned at that. "I happen to like turtles."

Cole managed something between a yawn and a gig-gle. "You like cars."

"I like cars and turtles. And hamburgers and little boys who go to sleep when they're supposed to."

"I like cars, too." Cole was so eager to connect with him.

Jake made his voice comically serious. "Cars, huh? Well, I'm not getting you one." In truth, there was nothing Jake would deny Cole right now. The kid could have asked for a pony—or a Ford Mustang for that matter—and Jake probably would have found a way.

Cole getting a sports car before he got one himself—wouldn't that be a laugh? The confirmed bachelor who was saving up for a dream cross-country drive in a restored '57 Chevy emptying his bank account to buy a Ford for a five-year-old. It wouldn't be any stranger than what had turned his life upside down already.

"Well, not for another eleven years, at least, so don't be asking. But Sanders men are Chevy men, so maybe we'll go look at some snazzy wheels when you turn fourteen or so and…"

Jake looked down at his nephew. Cole's breathing had finally, finally settled down into the soft rhythms of sleep. The boy was out.

Yawning himself, Jake carefully slipped his cell phone out of his pocket and pulled up Emma Mullins's number. Just as he felt himself drifting off, he typed a text message: Thanks. Really. I couldn't have done today without you. And I still owe you a burger. I owe you a lot.

Chapter Six

Emma's college friend Celia offered a frown to the Christmas decorations bursting from every corner of the Denver teahouse where they were meeting that Saturday afternoon. "I wish they'd wait until after Thanksgiving. It's becoming an invisible holiday—decor-wise, at least. But the food? That'll be with us forever." As an interior designer, Celia often had strong opinions on such things.

"Thanksgiving is days away. And it's late this year. So I guess the retailers need to get a jump on things. I know I feel like I haven't got enough time to get ready."

Celia chose from among the pretty cookies that graced a three-tiered stand between them. "The nativity thing *and* the library? Why'd Zosia do that to you?"

"It was a preschool board decision." Emma selected one of the little petit fours decorated to look like a Christmas present. "Well, actually, it was one member of the preschool board convincing the others. Norma Binton wants her niece to get the director job, so I think she's setting me up to fail because I'm Zosia's choice."

"That's pretty underhanded." Celia took a bite of the

rich-looking treat and moaned her delight. "But you can handle it. You're the most organized person I know."

"Well, I could, before Cole."

"That little boy? That is so sad. Heartbreaking." Celia raised her elegant teacup from its saucer and took a sip. "How's the little guy holding up?"

"As well as anyone can hope, I suppose. His bachelor uncle was only supposed to watch him for a week or so while the grandmother was packing up to move from Arizona. Only she fell and broke her ankle, so Jake has to step in for longer."

Celia seemed to take stock of whatever look Emma must have had on her face. "Bachelor Uncle Jake, huh? Rather deep waters for a novice parent, wouldn't you say?"

"Jake cares a lot about his nephew. He's just..." Emma searched for the right word "...lacking in steadiness."

"Oh," Celia said as understanding dawned in her wide brown eyes. "The *fun* kind of uncle. A cereal-for-dinner, stay-up-late, drink-milk-out-of-the-carton kind of uncle."

Emma laughed at the caricature. "Well, he's not that bad. I admire how hard he's trying. But he's grieving, too. The more time I spend with him, the more he surprises me. There's a lot going on under that fun uncle persona. I don't think he'll admit to anyone how much he cares or how lost he feels." She thought about the way Jake had looked at her as they drove to the urgent care center the other night. "At least to anyone but me."

Emma felt Celia studying her expression. "The way you're talking, I'm wondering just how charming and handsome is this bachelor uncle?"

"It's not like that," Emma refuted quickly. "I mean, he is charming and handsome...but... Jake and I? No."

"But it *could* be like that?" Celia pressed. "You don't sound too convinced of that *no*." Emma's friend had always been far too astute. "You're spending time together dealing with Cole, yes? Would it be so bad if there was something in it for you?"

"I'll admit, there are lots of women who'd consider Jake a catch. He's kind and bold and incredibly committed to helping Cole. I've never met anyone like him."

"So why not? He's clearly caught your eye. And from where I sit, that hasn't happened in a long time. You like the guy. Act on it."

"Under any other circumstances, maybe. But not with the way things are now. Norma Binton would pounce on it. He's the guardian of one of my students. It's not appropriate."

Celia leaned in on one elbow, unfazed. "You won't get off that easy. I still want to know more about him. Come on, what's this Jake guy like?"

Emma settled for the most complicated answer to that question. "Honestly, he strikes me as the kind of man Sam should have grown up to be."

That stopped Celia in her tracks, the way Emma had known it would. After a pause where she ran a manicured finger over her teacup handle, Celia asked, "Ah, so Jake is not the reason we're meeting here and not in Wander Canyon. Sam is." She gave Emma a concerned look. "Has he surfaced? Have you heard from him?"

There were very few people in Emma's life now who knew about Sam. Certainly no one in Wander Canyon. Celia knew this wasn't a conversation Emma could have had in Wander. Even the hour drive into Denver felt too close.

In reply, Emma reached into her handbag and pulled

out the four postcards she'd received from her brother over the past two months. They weren't signed and contained no words. Just drawings of landscapes, roads, trees and other scenes, each with one garish bit of bright red. They were simple drawings, black ink on white card stock. Each had Sam's artistic skill, but each also somehow bore his dark, confused nature.

Celia's gaze swept over the four cards. Could she see, as Emma could, that they grew darker, the lines more bold, the red increasing with each card? Sam was trying to tell her something, but Emma didn't know what. The old ache of guilt had started up again.

Her friend sighed. "Don't go there, Em. He didn't want your help. You couldn't have stopped him from checking himself out of that place."

Emma didn't reply. What had she come here to get from Celia? Another round of absolution? Just for someone else to see these and tell her what to do with them?

Celia turned the postcards over just as Emma had done, peering at the dates and locations on the postmarks. "So he's still out there wandering. I mean, these are from all over the state. He's not near you."

"I don't know that he sends them in any particular order. I don't know if he mails them right after he makes them. I don't know anything." Emma wished her voice hadn't tightened up so much on those last words.

"That's because he doesn't want you to." Celia put her hand on Emma's. "Look, you tried. Hard. You kept on with him even when he was so awful to you. You did everything you could, but he was just…lost."

"Did I?" Emma asked, the question catching, thick and painful, in her throat. "Isn't there always more? Why would he send me these if he isn't looking for more?"

Celia picked up one of the cards, flipping it to show both sides to Emma. "There's no signature. No information, no way for you to get in touch with him." She put the card back down, the four stark drawings looking odd against the soft elegance of the table setting. "Maybe this is just his way of telling you he's okay." She nodded toward the cards, shrugging as she did so. "Confused, rather off-kilter, but alive and well."

Emma stared at the pictures. "These don't look like they came from someone who's *well* to me."

"Sam hasn't been well since you two were kids. This is him. I suppose you could hire a private investigator or something, but are they really going to tell you anything you don't already know?"

Celia was right. Sam had stopped being a brother years ago. He'd become an emotional parasite of sorts, pulling all the energy and joy out of her anytime she dared to go visit him and leaving her with nothing but questions and regrets. On his good days, he barely spoke to her. On his bad days, he'd yell the most horrible accusations. He'd berate her for not saving him from whatever had sent him down this path, even though he was older and they were mere children when he'd started to slide.

"You did the right thing, Emma. You used to be torn apart for days after you saw him. You've been the happiest I've ever seen you this past year. Don't let Sam take that away. He doesn't deserve it. And maybe, in his own weird Sam way, he's happy. Maybe that's what he's trying to tell you."

Emma looked at the postcards again, searching the lines on the paper for any sign of peace or well-being. If it was there, she didn't see it. Or couldn't.

"What are you doing for Thanksgiving?" Celia asked, pouring more tea for them both.

"Me? Sewing Wise Men costumes, I suppose." In her head, she heard Jake's "wise guys" term for the Magi. It stuck with her so strongly, she half worried she'd call them *the wise guys* in front of Pastor Newton.

Celia made a face. "Doesn't every church have a battalion of grandmothers for that sort of thing?"

Emma laughed again. Celia's humor was always the best balm for any trouble. "I think they're tapped out from filling Jake's fridge with casseroles. And they're all with their own families, I'm sure."

"So come be with ours. Bring your sewing machine if you have to. None of us are crafty, but I'm sure we can help with hems or buttons or something." Celia had a warm, wonderful family with generous parents and two boisterous brothers. They'd included Emma in numerous family holidays through college and even after. Dad was good for a Christmas card, sometimes even with a fifty-dollar bill inside, but not for much else.

"I'm not taking no for an answer. Don't make me drive up to Wander and put you and your arts and crafts in my car." Celia raised an eyebrow and leaned in. "Then again, maybe I should come up and get a look at this fun bachelor uncle so I can help convince you to…"

"Okay!" Emma cut off any scheme Celia was cooking up. "I'll come. I'll bring a pie from our local bakery and a box of costume supplies."

"Good," Celia said. "Now put those cards away and let's finish off that pair of fudge tarts."

Jake swallowed hard at the figure on the paper Pastor Newton handed him after services on Sunday morning.

The pastor had grabbed Jake, Bo Carter and Emma for what he called "a brief spur-of-the-moment meeting" in his office. Cole had improved enough from his "giant bump," as he called it, to attend this morning's church service and was snacking on a pair of cookies the reverend had brought him.

Pastor Newton made a show of admiring Cole's trio of butterfly bandages. "Quite a shiner you've got there. Glad you've recovered enough to join us today."

"I could have done without the extra excitement," Jake admitted. Still, he was glad Cole seemed to recover fast and was even just a bit proud of his "tough-guy scar."

"I hear you. Well, I won't keep you long. I'm hoping you'll give us your approval to use the memorial funds donated on behalf of your sister and brother-in-law to buy children's books for the library expansion," Pastor Newton said. "I can't think of a better place for the money to go, can you?"

He ought to be grateful, but a fresh wave of loss flooded over Jake. All those donors. All that money. So many people loved Natalie and Kurt. How on earth could they be gone? What possible purpose was served by their lives being cut short like this? *I'll never get it, Lord*, Jake thought with more anger than he cared to admit. *You could come down on a cloud of glory and explain it to me right now and I'd still never get it.*

Cole peered over at the paper. "Is that a lot?"

"Yeah, buddy." Jake managed to get the words out. "It's a lot." The emotion in his voice brought Emma's gaze up to meet his. Her eyes just plain did things to him. They had a way of holding him steady, as if her gaze could send him some of the gentle patience she seemed to have so much of. Patience he was sorely lacking. He couldn't shake the notion that she saw right through to his bottled-up feelings. It partly bugged him. But mostly it drew him in. Things felt out of sorts when she wasn't around.

Bo, good friend and partner that he was, stepped in. "It means we'll be able to fill this library up, right? Just like your mom and dad would have wanted it. And you and all your friends can come get lots of books whenever you want."

"I like books," Cole said. "Lots'll be good."

"It does mean the job will be a bit bigger than we originally planned," Bo said. "But if you ask me, that's a happy problem. We can work to flesh out our initial plans. And Car-San Construction will kick in for the rest of the materials. We owe it to Natalie and Kurt."

The conversation went on, something about which wall was going to be knocked out and how far into the next room the new library would go. The words seemed to waft by Jake, out of reach behind a mist of thoughts about his sister and how she wouldn't be here to see any of it. She'd told him she wanted to buy big, squishy chairs to put in the library so moms could cuddle with their little ones and read together. Cole wouldn't get that chance, now or ever. Oh, he did his best to read books to Cole, but it wasn't the same. How could it be?

"Jake?" Pastor Newton's voice pulled him back.

"Huh?"

"I was wondering how soon after the holidays you wanted to get started. We'll want to shift some things around."

The impulse hit him as strong as the grief. "Now. I want to get started now."

Pastor Newton sat back. "There's no rush, son. The holidays are practically here already."

That was exactly why he needed to get started now. Didn't they see that? "I want to get started on this right away."

"Give us a week to finish up Joe Harrison's addition, and then we'll get you some drawings." Bo used his businesslike tone of voice.

Only this wasn't a business decision. This was survival. This library project felt like the only way Jake was going to hang on to his sanity through all the coming holiday happiness. "Nat's birthday was December thirtieth. I'd want the library to be open by then."

The cautious looks around the table dug under Jake's skin. "Isn't that rather...ambitious?" Pastor Newton asked.

"We don't need it that quickly," Emma added.

"I do." Jake put the force of everything burning in his gut behind the two words.

"I was gonna buy her a book for her birthday," Cole said, oblivious to the friction in the room. "Now we can get her a whole libary."

Jake glared around the table, daring even one of them to correct his nephew's pronunciation. "What he said."

Bo ran one hand down his face. "Okay, Pastor, I guess Jake and I will pull together some ideas and get back to you next week."

Jake eyed his partner. "I'll have drawings for you in two days." He wasn't sleeping anyhow, so why not put the long nights to good use?

"There's no need to rush this, Jake." Emma had her teacher voice on now. This was supposed to be his project. Natalie had asked him to do it. It had been the last thing she'd asked him. Besides, Emma had said she needed to impress the preschool board committee, and he was sitting here handing her a way to do it. Why was everyone ganging up against him on this?

"It'll be ready by Nat's birthday."

"I don't see any reason to decide this right now." The pastor stood up. "Jake, whenever you get those drawings to me will be soon enough. Take your time. You've got a lot on your plate."

"So everybody keeps saying," Jake shot back. Everyone was telling him to slow down, but every time he did, the gaping hole of loss rose up and threatened to swallow him.

"You can do it, Uncle Jake," Cole chimed in. "I'll help."

The bandages still peeking out from Cole's cowlick probably said something to the wisdom of that, but Jake would find a way for the little guy to help. They ought to do this together. This should be Cole's win as much as it was his.

Emma probably thought Jake hadn't seen the look that flashed between herself and the reverend. "Didn't you say you still owed me a burger?" she asked brightly. "I need to pick up some art supplies over by the mall. What do you say the three of us—you, me and Cole—head to Chevy's and talk over ideas?"

"Talk some sense into this guy, will you?" Bo half joked, sounding like he wasn't really joking at all. It didn't take a genius to know Jake was reaching the end of Bo's patience. Given the choice between a lecture from Bo or one from Emma, he was going to opt for the pretty lady and a good burger.

"Thanks. That sounds great."

"Chevy's? Hooray!" Cole shouted, scrambling for his coat. The retro diner, famous for their milkshakes, was always a favorite of his.

"I'll check back with you later this afternoon, Pastor," Emma said as she reached for her coat. She was probably going to try to talk Jake out of this idea, but that wasn't happening. This project was the lifeline that was going to get him and Cole through the holidays. It felt like the first solid thing he'd grabbed on to in a sea of sadness. Hadn't Pastor Newton told him to trust his gut in finding ways to deal with his grief? To "go with the ebb and flow of his feelings"? This was the first time he felt a flow instead of a continual ebb.

He may owe Emma a burger, but he owed Natalie the library. And he owed Cole a chance to see one little piece of the world set right.

Chapter Seven

Cole tugged on Jake's hand—something that never failed to raise a sentimental lump in his throat—as they walked over to a red "convertible" booth in Chevy's Diner a short time later. "Look, Uncle Jake, we're gonna sit in your car!"

"Well, aren't you smart to see that," Jake replied.

Jake's car was actually a '57 Chevy rather than the generalized 50s-style convertible of the booth, but he appreciated Cole's effort. Would that trip ever happen now? Or would it be one of a thousand things that wouldn't be the way he planned now that Natalie was gone?

"The car for your big road trip?" Emma asked. Cole must have told her about it, and she remembered. He'd heard her spout dozens of little details like that about the people around her. It pleased him that she'd remembered this one.

Besides, he'd much rather talk about his dream car than whatever Emma had in mind. "Well, no car's mine at the moment."

"Gonna be," Cole said with pint-size confidence.

"Someday." Jake hoisted his nephew onto a small

booster seat the server brought and slid in beside the boy. "I've got my eye on a few contenders. Fifty-seven Chevys in good enough shape to make the trip I have in mind don't come cheap."

"He's gonna drive all the way across the country and send me stuff from every place," Cole said.

"You told me," Emma said with a sweet smile. "It sounds like an amazing adventure."

"I planned to take Route 66 clear through to Santa Monica and send Cole postcards from every stop. Nat was going to make a book of all the postcards." It still stung to talk about his sister in the past tense. There seemed to be a million things Natalie had been going to do that now would never happen.

"You should still do that," Emma offered. She really must have some kind of preschool-issue mind-reading superpowers. She was always saying things that made him sure she could read his thoughts. He admired that she paid attention to everyone, but he especially liked that she paid attention to him. "It's a great idea," she went on, looking as if she genuinely liked the idea when most people found it a bit crazy. "Hardly anyone ever sends honest-to-goodness postcards anymore."

"Maybe," Jake replied, trying not to let his tone sink despite the weight he felt in his chest. "But that particular adventure is off the table. At least for now."

"'Cuz of the libary?" Cole asked.

Emma raised an eyebrow at Jake. Maybe she was thinking Cole's remark would somehow soften his conviction for the library's speedy timetable. *Nope. Not happening, Miss Emma.*

"Because of a lot of things."

Emma opened her menu. "Well, I think it sounds like

a fun idea. Who wouldn't want to take an adventure like that? You should do it…someday."

"What adventure would you want to take if you had the chance?" He discovered he really wanted to know. She was so interested in other people, but so careful and cautious with people's interest in her. He wanted to find the woman behind that soft-but-thick wall she threw up around herself.

"Oh, no. Not me. I'm not the adventure type."

He gave her a slanted grin. "Maybe you just haven't met the right adventure."

She threw him a look that told him she recognized that for the cheap line it was. She was right. She was better than the usual tactics he used on women.

Jake waited for her to cut the small talk and launch into whatever lecture she had planned, but she simply scanned the menu. He opted to beat her to the punch.

"Are you here to talk me out of the library timetable?"

Emma's eyes flashed toward Cole and back to Jake as if to say *do you really want to have that conversation right now?* She adopted an innocent smile. "I'm here because you owe me a burger."

"And you said I get a milkshake, right?" Cole insisted.

"I keep my promises, little man."

When the server came and took their orders, she offered Cole a coloring place mat and a small pack of crayons. "Can we all have one?" Emma asked.

The server gave Emma the same odd expression Jake did. "Huh?"

"Coloring is great for the soul," she replied. When the server returned with two more sets of place mats and crayons, Emma opened her packet of crayons and began working as if grown-ups colored kiddie place mats every day.

Cole pushed Jake's little box of crayons toward him. "C'mon, Uncle Jake, do one, too."

Jake thought Emma was off her rocker, but he didn't see any other option than to select a red crayon and begin filling in a spot on the place mat. *This is silly*, he thought as he watched Cole settle happily into the task, his little tongue sticking out in creative intensity. After a minute or two of them all coloring, Emma turned her place mat over, wrote something in crayon and slid it across the table. *You're not okay, are you?*

Jake didn't know which impressed him more—her brilliance at finding a way to have the conversation she wanted without Cole hearing, or the gutsy meddling nature of her question. Nosy as it was, it still was far better than the onslaught of "How *are* you?"s he regularly endured.

"Should I make the kitty orange or blue?" Cole asked Jake.

"I've always thought cats should come in blue," Jake replied. "It's a cool color."

"But your special car's gonna be red."

"My special car's gonna be whatever color I can afford first."

"Mom and Dad's car was red." Cole said it so matter-of-factly it burned a hole in Jake's chest.

Emma seemed to have a weird reaction to that detail. Which wasn't that odd—lots of people got uncomfortable when Cole brought up the accident. Jake kept trying to accept any of the boy's death-related comments as natural conversation, but it was like swallowing a fishhook, snagging and ripping at his insides. "Yeah," he said, lost for any other reply. "It was."

"So you should get a red one. Like Mom and Dad had." The words seemed to weigh a hundred pounds, but Cole said them with a weightless innocence.

Jake stared at Emma for a moment, groping for some clue as to how he was supposed to handle stuff like this. Be casual? Be serious? Who on earth knew? He decided if Emma was going to go the distance to pry, he was going to give her the real answer. *NO*, he wrote back to the question still staring at him from the overturned place mat. *Not even close.*

Emma pulled the menu back to her side and read it. He watched it register in her eyes, absurdly grateful for the silent connection. She knew what this was like. She got him, got Cole, and that was worth a lot. The ease between them was so rare for him these days. He didn't have to try to explain himself or say the right thing in front of her.

Jake allowed himself the momentary luxury of a long look into her eyes. Their sky blue color felt spacious and peaceful to him. He enjoyed the way they squinted up just a bit when she smiled or laughed, and felt a pang that neither of them had had much reason to do either lately. Maybe, when all this was over—if it was ever truly over—he'd find a way to keep that sweet smile on her face.

After a moment, the connection between them grew too close. Emma broke his gaze and turned to Cole. "I want to give my cat brown stripes. What do you think?"

"Otto and Oscar have stripes," Cole reminded her. "I like stripes."

She colored for a bit on the drawing side of the place mat, then turned it over for another message to Jake.

You can't rush this. It doesn't work that way, came the crayon message across the paper place mat.

Whether she was talking about the library job or his "grief journey," as Pastor Newton liked to call it, Jake didn't have any choice but to rush it. He was trying to outrun the black cloud coming for him. Any way he kept ahead of it was a good idea as far as he was concerned. *I can do it*, he wrote back. He didn't have to specify.

He shouldn't have found her exasperated look so amusing. Nat probably would have chided him for goading someone who was just trying to help. But as much as he liked Emma nearby and thinking about him rather than just about Cole, that closeness came at the price of her poking at his raw spots.

I can and I will, he added before pushing the paper back toward her in a *that settles it* motion. He considered it God's personal grace when the server came back with their milkshakes and the place mats had to be put to their intended uses.

Emma backed down with her words, but not with her eyes. That woman had what his grandmother would have called "gumption."

"Have you thought about the stable?" she asked.

Oh, she had gumption, all right. He couldn't very well skimp on her stable while he was asking for her cooperation on the library. "Easy peasy. We build a back wall of old barn wood, a small roof of straw over one-by-two so it doesn't weigh much and brace the whole thing up from the back so there's room for the people in front. The fencing should help it stay steady if there's wind."

"Fencing?"

"Well, you're going to have animals, aren't you? You can't have live people and fake animals."

The look on her face told him that was exactly what she had planned. "You're surrounded by ranches. You've got a ready supply of cattle, sheep, donkeys...you're gonna need a fence. And a good one. You don't want a repeat of what happened two years ago."

Her eyes went wide. "What happened two years ago?"

Jake found himself enjoying a delightful dilemma. The hysterical story would surely make her laugh—and he wanted to see the sparkle come back to her eyes— but he also didn't want to give her new reasons to worry. "I'll simply advise you to ask the locals for the most docile animal they've got. And to feed them well before showtime."

Emma narrowed one eye. "Why do I get the feeling there's way more to that story?"

Cole chose to answer for him. "The goat ate some- body's costume and ran down the street. Mom told me about it. Everybody laughed." That year's goat had, in fact, eaten an alarming portion of Joseph's costume and promptly jumped the fence with the remainder, drag- ging it down the street with a dozen congregants in hot pursuit. He couldn't believe someone hadn't already told her. Norma Binton must really be trying to set her up for failure. Talk about feisty old goats...

"Okay," Emma said as their food arrived. "I want a full rundown of past nativity disasters and how you think I can avoid them."

"Ah, so that's why you really came to lunch," Jake teased. She was fun to tease, and fun had felt like such foreign territory lately. "You need intel."

She'd been outmaneuvered and she knew it. "You got me." The smiles they shared struck a small glow in Jake's gut. An out-of-place glow, maybe, but definitely not one he wanted to tamp down anytime soon.

Cole simply sipped his milkshake. "You guys are silly."

Monday morning after dropping off Cole, Jake headed over to Car-San to put in a solid day's work. The moment he walked into the office, however, it became clear that wasn't going to happen. Bo stood at the door, pointing to a set of chairs. "Sit."

Bo didn't bark orders often, so Jake knew better than to argue. He took a seat.

Bo sat down opposite him. "What was yesterday all about?"

"The meeting at church?"

"Yes, the meeting at church. The one where you boxed yourself into an impossible project."

Jake leaned his elbows on his knees. "It's not impossible."

"It's close." Bo leaned back and crossed his arms over his chest. "On top of the holidays? Tear up the church hallways at Christmas? You're not thinking this through."

Bo wasn't saying anything Jake didn't already know. It wasn't ideal. It probably wasn't even smart. But none of that mattered in the face of the bone-deep desperation he felt to get it done. So he chose the only defense he had. "It's not like you haven't done something like this." Bo had, in fact, taken on an ill-advised job a year ago when he signed on to help Toni Redding overhaul her family's general store. "And I recall it turning out pretty good." Toni and Bo had been high school sweethearts, and the project reunited them. Jake had been the best man at their wedding this past summer.

"I…we…had the time. I wasn't juggling twelve other crises at the time. I hadn't just buried someone who meant the world to me." Bo softened his voice. "Come on, Jake, you completely missed the permit deadlines for the Byers job this week. You're not all here, even when you're here."

A burst of defensiveness crawled up Jake's spine. "So that's what this is about. As if you've never missed a permit deadline, huh?" The minute he snapped that out, Jake knew that wasn't fair. The recent pile-on of people telling him to be sensible was getting to him.

Bo pressed his lips together. "I'm gonna let that go. This isn't about work, and you know it. This is about you. You're about to run off the rails, buddy, and I'm just trying to yank you back."

Jake stood up and walked over to the supply shelves. He and Bo had been friends a long time. If anyone had earned the right to call him on something, it was Bo. But he wasn't going to give Bo—or anyone else, for that matter—the option to do it.

"Cole needs you," came Bo's quiet insistence from behind Jake.

"That's just it." Jake turned back to face his friend. "He's counting on me to find some way to get him through Thanksgiving and Christmas with no family. How on earth am I supposed to do that? How on earth am I supposed to make it anything other than terrible and awful?" He didn't like that his throat caught on the words, even in front of Bo. When was he ever going to feel anything close to his normal self, able to laugh and crack jokes and roll with life the way he used to?

"I don't know, but I'm pretty sure the answer isn't to build a library."

"I can't think of anything else. At least this will give

Cole and me something to do other than sit around and think about everyone who isn't here." Jake ran his hands down his face, struggling to explain something he simply knew. "I gotta do this. You don't have to tell me it's insane. I already know that." It struck him, right at that moment, that there was one important thing he hadn't done yet. "So I'm asking you to help me, okay? Help me do this."

Bo walked over and put a hand on Jake's shoulder. "You know I will. But someone should tell you it's insane, even if you do already know it."

Jake hadn't expected the relief that hit him to feel so strong. He needed Bo on his side. With Natalie gone, he'd felt like one of the anchors that held him steady had snapped its line and set him adrift. Rather than try to come up with a bigger word than *thanks*, he simply nodded. "I'll go file the Byers permits now and pay the late fine out of my own pocket."

"Already done," Bo said. "I covered for you. 'Cause that's what partners are for." He paused, and Jake thought they were done with this little partners meeting until Bo said, "So, let's talk about Emma."

Maybe he hadn't hidden his interest in her as well as he thought. At least not to someone who knew him as well as Bo. He didn't need a second lecture on insane ideas this morning. "Let's *not* talk about Emma."

Bo widened his stance. "Oh, no. We're gonna talk about Emma."

He tried dodging the conversation. "She's helping out with Cole. Which I desperately need, so I'm grateful."

Bo leaned back against a supply cabinet, crossing one boot over the other. "Nope."

Jake began flipping through a supply list for the afternoon's job. He wasn't sure he had it in him right now to talk about how she was getting under his skin. "Gimme a break, will you? You just got done telling me I'm in over my head."

"Yeah, and I'm thinking this might be a different kind of in over your head." Bo began pulling supplies out of the cabinet. "You like her."

Even though he knew it was probably useless, Jake tried shifting the statement around. "I'm grateful to her."

"Maybe, but there's more to it. And that's not a bad thing. Although, the timing worries me. What's going on with you two?"

Bo's persistence could be annoying at times. "Okay, maybe there's a bit more than that. She's the one person who doesn't make me feel like I'm in over my head. With Cole, that is."

"Didn't you tell me otherwise? That she was helping you out because she thought you weren't up to taking care of Cole?"

"Well, yeah, that's what I thought. One more voice in the 'Poor Jake, he has no idea what to do' choir."

"But she's not. She's…" Bo raised an eyebrow. "Maybe something else entirely?"

Should he admit what he was starting to feel for her? Was he ready to do that? His feelings were such a useless tangle, he wasn't ready to trust what he felt about anything right now. Yet Emma seemed different. She *was* different. "I don't know," he began, reaching for some way to explain it. "She has a way of making me feel like I might be okay at this. Like I'm exactly who Cole needs." Jake shook his head. "Ignore my rambling."

Bo stilled. "I do think you're exactly who Cole needs. I think Emma's right."

Jake began pulling coils of wire off the shelf. "You and nobody else."

"So the library is to prove everyone wrong?"

At least Bo had pivoted off the topic of Emma Mullins. "Interesting theory, Dr. Carter, but no." He tossed the coils into a box. "You know how much stock I put in what other people think."

Bo pointed a finger at Jake. "But you care what Emma thinks. Of you. What if she's exactly what you need?"

"Well, yeah, I need her *help*." That somehow felt safer than saying he needed *her*, which is how he was starting to feel. But even admitting he needed her help felt like a gigantic step.

"Coming clean that he needs somebody's help." Bo's knowing tone was annoying. "Strange new territory for the likes of Jake Sanders."

Jake turned to look at Bo. "Being married has made you really annoying, you know that?"

Bo made a gooey face and put one hand over his chest. "I love you, too, man. And you're still coming to the house for Thanksgiving."

"Feeling the love," Jake muttered as he punched the button that opened the metal garage door to reveal where he'd backed in his truck. "Are we done here? Some of us have work to do."

"I don't know. Are you going to show them to me?"

"Show you what?" Jake asked over his shoulder as he lowered the tailgate on his truck.

"These library plans you're about to stay up all night to pull together. Somebody's got to draw up a budget for them, and we all know how you rot at that."

Bo knew him better than anyone—except for Nat. His

friend's comment was as close to an "I'm in," as Jake needed. "We can go over them at Thanksgiving."

"Roast turkey with a side of library budget," Bo joked. "What could be more fun than that?"

Chapter Eight

Jake walked into the house on Wednesday afternoon, and the scent that hit him filled him with relief. "You managed it?" he called as he headed into the kitchen to say a huge thank-you to Emma. She'd saved him from certain embarrassment.

His relief dipped a bit at the state of the space. Evidently baking with a five-year-old could destroy a kitchen in a single afternoon. "Well," offered Emma as she finished wiping down a cabinet, "barely managed it. The pie crust just about did us in."

"We made a pie!" Cole announced with enough glee to make Jake wonder if he hadn't just launched a chef's career. The boy held up sticky fingers smeared with flour and what Jake hoped was pumpkin.

Jake high-fived him anyway. "Just like we promised Mr. Bo and Mrs. Toni." It still amazed him that Bo and Toni were now Mr. and Mrs. even though he couldn't think of two people who deserved it more.

"I thought we were goners when the bakery said they only had enough left to fill preorders." Jake looked at

Emma. "I couldn't really stand the thought of showing up at Thanksgiving with a cherry pie. It's wrong, somehow."

"I like cherry pie, too," Cole offered, then turned to Emma. "Can we make one of those next?"

Emma wrung out a dish towel. "How about we wait a week to get all the mess from this one out of the kitchen?"

Jake took the wet towel from her, aware of their fingers touching when he did. She had the most adorable smudge of flour on her chin, and against his better judgment he wiped it off for her. The startled look in her eyes didn't entirely cover the warmth in them at his gesture. The softness of her face threw him off balance, and it took him a second to recover. "I'll take care of the disaster mitigation. I owe you that much."

Emma tried to shrug as if what had just happened was no big deal. "It gave us something nice to do. School was a bit crazy today with the kids all hyped up for the holiday."

Cole held up a construction paper turkey made from his handprint. "We made turkeys."

Jake hunched down to appreciate the artwork. "I remember making one of those when I was your age. We should put it on the fridge, right?" Natalie was always putting Cole's artwork—even when it was just toddler smudges of finger paint—on the fridge. Was this the first time someone other than Nat had done this for Cole? It was the first time he'd done it, and a little pang stung his heart when he fixed the turkey to the fridge with one of the colorful alphabet magnets. "Looks great," he managed, the words thick enough to pull a sad smile from Emma.

She rinsed her hands in the sink. "The pie will be

ready in ten minutes. Just put it on the rack I set out and slip it in the fridge when it cools off."

"Seriously, I can't thank you enough. I hope we got you out of here in time to make it to your friend's without hitting too much traffic."

Her face fell. "Oh, that's not an issue anymore. Both of Celia's parents came down with the flu. I'll be steering clear of those germs, thank you very much."

"So what are you going to do?"

She began gathering her bag. "I'll be tucked in at home making serious progress on nativity costumes. It'll be great to catch up since I'm behind schedule and the woman who was supposed to make the shepherd robes came down with whatever bug is going around."

"Alone?" Jake balked.

Cole seemed to find that just as unacceptable. "You can't be nowhere on Thanksgiving!"

Emma laughed. "I won't be nowhere. I'll be at home, getting important things done."

It wasn't even a decision. "Nope. That won't fly. Not with me, not after you just made me a pie. I'll call Bo and you can go over to his house with us."

"You can't just invite me over to someone else's house on short notice," Emma protested.

"This isn't someone, this is Bo. I know he and Toni will say yes. Bring the costumes. Toni's the crafty sort. We'll all pitch in and you won't be alone." When she opened her mouth to refuse, he stopped her. Finally, the chance to do something for her instead of the other way around. "Don't even try and say no."

Cole grabbed her arm. "You gotta come. You gotta."

"You're outnumbered. And I know where you live."

That sounded a bit wrong to admit, so he added, "I'll come fetch you if you don't show. You know I will."

He even liked the way she narrowed her eyes at him. "Do you always get your way?"

He knew he had her. "Most times." Tomorrow would be so much better with her coming along. The gaping hole left by Kurt and Natalie would feel smaller. She'd know how to handle the million awkward moments he and Cole would have making their way through their first Thanksgiving without Nat and Kurt. He'd been panicked all week about what tomorrow would feel like, even with Bo and Toni, and he felt the dread settle down a notch. More than a notch. "So that's a yes?"

"I don't have much choice, do I?" The reluctance in her words never quite reached her eyes.

"Nope," said Cole, yanking on her hand as if he could pull the agreement out of her fingers.

"Okay, then. I'll come. But only if Bo and Toni say it's okay."

"Hooray!" Cole did a silly dance, looking just as giddy as Jake felt at the flickering in his own chest.

"They'll say yes." To prove his point, Jake pulled out his cell phone and hit the contact info for Bo. When his partner answered, Jake put the phone on speaker and said, "Emma just made a pie for us and her own plans tanked out so she's coming with us tomorrow. That's fine, right?"

Emma rolled her eyes, her cheeks turning that memorable shade of pink again.

"Absolutely," came Bo's voice.

"She's totally welcome," came Toni's voice from the background. "Especially since Bo says you…"

Jake tapped off the speakerphone function as fast as his fingers could move, not wanting to broadcast whatever meddling Toni was about to launch. "Told you it'd be fine," he said to cover the cutoff, but it was too late. Emma had turned away, but even the set of her shoulders told him she'd already guessed that he'd been talking to Bo about her. He said a quick goodbye and signed off the call.

"They have a dog," Cole said, saving both of them from acknowledging what had just happened. "His name is Dodger and he plays fetch and his ears are really soft."

"I mean it about the costumes," Jake added. "Why is it I've got people lining up to give me casseroles I don't need and you're stuck doing most of the nativity work yourself?"

"Norma's pushing to expand the preschool director's position into handling all the children's ministries for the church. She wants the position to be larger for her niece, I suppose. Or just to prove I can't do it and her niece can. Evidently, her niece has a master's in ministry, and I only have a bachelor's in early childhood education." Her lips pressed together, as if she'd admitted more than she cared to in front of Cole. Still, it was clear to Jake that if Norma meant to put the squeeze on Emma, Old Biddy Binton was succeeding. The urge to stomp over there and give Norma a piece of his mind rose up in Jake's gut. He wasn't normally the protective hero type, but this was Emma. Facing Norma. Even Nat hadn't liked Norma, and Nat liked everybody.

"This year's live nativity is going to blow all the others out of the water. You watch." It wasn't exactly Emma's brand of sweet encouragement, but he wanted her to know he was on her side. "I'll have the stable built early, just to take the wind out of her sails."

"Joshua said we're gonna have a camel this year," Cole piped up. "Are we really?"

Wouldn't that shut Norma's plans down? Jake scratched his head. "Do I know anyone with a camel? Do you think the zoo would rent one out? I would fund that myself just to watch the look on Norma's face." Not exactly an admirable Christmas spirit, but it would feel great.

Emma's teacher voice returned. "This isn't a competition," she chided. Then she turned her attention to Cole. "A camel would be fun, but we'll just have to use our imagination. Maybe Joshua is forgetting that camels are from the desert, and they'd be cold in our canyon, don't you think?"

"We have lots of cows," Cole said. "They're here all winter."

"Sheep and cows and donkeys all like the winter here," Jake added, tamping down his competitive streak for Emma's sake. "And we can always add a goat or two."

"With a very good fence," Emma added.

"With the best fence I know how to build," Jake promised. Emma deserved nothing less.

Bo and Toni's house was decorated with perfect style, their fire was cozy, the meal had been spectacular. Given all that, Emma's heavy spirit should have disappeared. She hoped no one else had noticed, that she'd hidden her sadness and worry enough that neither Cole nor Jake nor her very gracious hosts would know. Cole didn't seem to catch on, nor did Bo and Toni.

Jake, on the other hand, was a different story. Somehow their connection had deepened yesterday in the kitchen. Over the beautiful table groaning with enough food to feed sixteen, never mind that they were only six, Emma kept catching Jake looking at her. The long, deep gaze he'd given her yesterday felt like it seeped clear out to her fingertips and made her feel startlingly close to him. He was surely trying twice as hard to keep up a good front for reasons everybody knew. It couldn't help but make her feel connected to him as a kindred spirit, even if no one else knew the reason.

Toni's father, Don, had launched into a rousing game of checkers with Cole by the fire. Bo and Toni talked quietly on the couch as they watched the match. The scene had *happy family* written all over it, which stung as much as it pleased Emma to view.

She walked over to stand in front of the windows that looked out across the grand mountains. Their size made her feel small, insignificant, which today was somehow comforting. Maybe it wouldn't matter that gratitude felt beyond her right now. Her bitter spirit could go unnoticed. Everyone else could be happy and thankful while she could wallow in the things—the people—that were absent.

Jake came up and stood next to her, staring out as well at the majestic view. "I keep thinking it ought to feel better," he said quietly. The quietness of his tone brought back the unwelcome memory of the gentle touch he'd given her cheek yesterday. She wished—mostly, but not completely—that he hadn't done that.

"Yeah," she said, although her sigh never really settled into the actual word.

He shifted his weight uncomfortably. "I need to get out of here for a bit. Want to take a walk?"

She hadn't realized until just that moment that it was the coziness of the place that weighed on her. Getting out under the open sky, the bright snow and fluffy clouds, felt like an excellent idea. Jake was in much the same place. He wouldn't be looking for her to be happy or productive. It let her welcome his companionship, even though it probably wasn't the wisest of ideas to be alone with him. They weren't at school; they weren't at church. This was just two friends walking out from under a burden while Cole had kind people to watch over him. "Sure," she replied. "That sounds great."

Bundled up, they walked out Toni and Bo's back door to a path that led off through a small patch of woods. The urge to hide in the trees hummed in her bones. She wanted to be a little bit lost, thinking of all she had lost, of how lost Sam must be.

Jake gave her the grace of silence until they reached the tall copse of birch trees poking straight and narrow up into the clear blue sky. "I know why I'm a grump," he said with a half-hearted smile. "But is there a reason why you look so down?"

"There's so much…family…in there." That was a cumbersome way to put it, but she knew he'd understand.

Jake turned up the collar of his coat and stuffed his hands in his pockets. "Kind of hard to choke down when you're missing those pieces, isn't it?" After walking a little farther, he asked, "Is your dad still around? You never said."

"We…don't talk anymore. Mom's death sort of—what was the word you used? Wrecked? It wrecked him in ways he couldn't find a way back from. Or just didn't want to."

Jake looked up at the sky. "It's almost worse when they can't be bothered, isn't it?" There was so much compassion in his tone. Kindred spirit, indeed. Celia was a wonderful friend, but Emma and Jake shared a depth of layered loss few people could understand.

"I don't think he knows how." It was the kindest way she could think of to describe the complicated tangle of her family. It wasn't even really a family. Just a loose collection of damaged souls tied by genetics and yet split by tragedy. "Can't really do family by yourself." The last word made her think of Sam. The previous postcards had made her guess him to be out wandering in some woods. The one that arrived last night had seemed less remote, and she didn't know what to make of that.

They walked on in more silence until Jake blurted out, "I miss Nat so much it's like my ribs are breaking from the inside. Somehow I'm hollow and stuffed to bursting at the same time."

His words were steeped in pain. Emma stopped walking and put a hand on his arm. If it had been anyone else she would have offered a hug, but she couldn't cross that line with Jake. "It won't hurt this bad next year," she consoled him, squeezing his arm. "It will always hurt, just not this bad."

Jake struggled to tamp his emotions back down after the sudden outburst. "Have you got a brother or sister? You never said."

Oh, what a loaded question that was. If she trod carefully, maybe she could talk about Sam just a bit, so far from everyone else back at the house. After all, she knew Jake would understand. She could trust him just enough to push the words up and out from the dark corner of her chest where they fought to stay hidden. "I have a brother. Sam. I don't talk about him." It ought to have echoed up against the mountain, the words felt so large to say out loud. "We're…we're not close." She felt like she had to add, "Anymore."

Given that he'd just lost his sister, Emma waited for some treasure-him-while-he's-still-here speech, but Jake merely looked at her, his own pain still glinting like sharp steel in the gray of his eyes, and asked, "Why?"

How to explain Sam? "Mom's death made Sam come…unglued. He's four years older than me, but he couldn't climb out of what happened to Mom any more than my dad could. He was worse, actually. He spiraled down into some dark place no one could pull him out of." Jake's eyes and the expanse of the space seemed to pull back the pain of talking about Sam. Instead, the words nearly raced to get out of her. "Depression, anxiety, it all just sort of took him away from us." She found a fallen tree trunk and sat down on it, suddenly feeling worn out. "He's a person, and still with us, but the person who was my big brother Sammy left when my mother did."

She was more grateful than wary when Jake sat down next to her. "Rough stuff," he said. "I didn't know."

"Nobody does. For years, I tried to keep up with him. Reach out, visit when he went to the group home, send letters."

"What would happen when you did?" Jake asked. Did that man realize what a gift it was for her not to hear even a hint of judgment in his voice?

"Occasionally, he would be sweet. Well, as sweet as he was capable of being. Nothing I'd ever call loving." She cast her gaze back in the direction of the familial bliss going on beside the fire in Bo and Toni's house. "Nothing like that."

"Kind of hard to swallow all that happiness today, isn't it?"

Emma nodded. "More often, Sam would lash out. Yell. Blame me, as if I could somehow stop what happened to him. He'd say the most terrible things. Finally I just stopped. Trying, that is." With him beside her, the thick, hard shell over that part of her heart cracked open, spilling the words out.

"I don't tell anyone because I'm ashamed of it." That might have been the first time she'd ever said that out loud, and the admission froze in her like the cold mountain air. "I know I should be strong enough to keep trying, but…"

"Hey, no," Jake said softly, putting his leather-gloved hand over the bright yellow knitted mittens she wore. Even through the layers, the intensity of the contact was as enormous as the mountain behind them. It startled her and called to her in equal measure. A tremendous urge to give in, to bury her face in his broad shoulder and sob, came out of nowhere. He had much more to grieve than she did. He was strong enough to pull himself—and Cole—up out of this valley. She wanted that strength. Wouldn't it be lovely to lean into it, just for today? Here, where nobody could watch or judge? Did she really have it in her to fight this connection between them that refused to stay behind appropriate lines?

"Emma…" He moved closer.

Panicked, Emma backed away from him and pushed up off the log. She wasn't entitled to this. "And I'll tell you something ugly. And awful. I'm relieved. How terrible is that? I can't handle the pain and stress of him anymore and I'm relieved." She stood a distance from him and spread her arms. "Can you imagine what Norma Binton would do with that bit of information?"

He stood up and began walking toward her, but she

stepped away. She urgently needed to put some space between them. "The truth is, I don't even know where Sam is right now. He left the group home in August. I've gotten a few postcards, but they don't even have words on them. No message, no phone number, nothing."

Jake took another step toward her. "I haven't talked to my father in eight years. And I *have* his phone number. Or at least the last one he bothered to give me." Jake's voice lowered, anger simmering in his eyes. "I don't call," he went on. "And I don't want to. Because he's a jerk and I can honestly say I haven't got a shred of love left for the guy. You tell me—does that make me a monster?"

No wonder the destruction of such a rich family life as Cole's was tearing him apart. Emma wiped her cheek with one mitten. "No."

"It makes me want to be sure Cole *never* feels like this. That he never feels as if the world couldn't care less about him. Ever."

Jake crossed the space between them and took her shoulders in his hands. While she should have stopped him, she didn't. She couldn't. She didn't want to. "It makes you care," he insisted, and the words wrapped his strength around her. "You care so much. And Cole needs that, so I'm glad that you do." He pulled her to him, and she didn't stop that, either. "I'm glad you care about us."

She should have corrected him, told him that her care for Cole's welfare was as his teacher, but that was no longer true. She did care about both of them. For just a moment, it felt so good to have someone hear the ugliest truth of her life and not be mortified. To be held, tenderly, after such a bruising admission.

This is Jake, she strove to remind herself. *This is the guardian of one of your students. This is not appropri-*

ate, no matter how it feels. So the instant she could gather enough strength to step away, she did.

"We should go back."

"Okay, yeah," he agreed, although she couldn't say if it was hurt or confusion that she saw in his eyes. She started walking toward the house, but he grabbed her hand. "Hey. I won't say a word to anyone about your brother. Know that, okay?"

"Thanks." He knew she needed that assurance and freely gave it to her. Her heart took that small consideration and held it tight. It occurred to her that even though she'd tried to make sure they never crossed a line toward each other, they just had.

Now she'd have to find a way to make sure it never happened again.

Chapter Nine

Jake felt bad about calling in late to work—again—but Bo would understand. When Chief Perkins asked him to stop by the police station the following Wednesday, Jake complied. Perkins said he had some news about Natalie and Kurt's deaths, and there was no way in the world Jake would delay a task like that.

Even so, part of him dreaded it. Was he about to learn they had a suspect in custody? Too much anger still simmered under his skin to know what he'd do once he learned who had fired that shot from the overpass. He couldn't imagine what sick soul aimed at random people in a speeding car, sending them anonymously to their deaths for no good reason. The whole thing shook his sense of justice. To be honest, it shook his faith that God was still sovereign over the broken world.

"I'll send up a few for you," Bo had said when Jake told him the reason for his absence. It was their shorthand for saying a situation needed prayer. And this one certainly did.

Bo had spent a bit too much time in the Wander Canyon police station during their high school days—Jake had pulled his friend back from the brink of delinquency more than once that summer after graduation when Toni broke Bo's heart into a million reckless pieces. Jake, however, had always steered just this side of trouble despite his inattentive mom and dad. Star pitcher on the baseball team, Jake could have easily taken any of the college offers he'd had after school. But he'd never been that sort. The idea of launching Car-San Construction with Bo was always his favored choice. And they'd done very well, even with Bo's "angry little detour," as Jake called it.

Now, Jake felt himself teetering on the edge of his own angry detour—and it didn't feel little at all. *Stick around, will You?* Jake prayed as he pushed open the doors of the cedar-shingled building with a row of tidy black-and-white police cars parked out front.

"Hey, Jake," Donna at the front desk said with a smile. Lots of people in a town as small as Wander Canyon knew everyone by name, but Jake had found it a sad commentary that most everyone in the police department could now recognize him on sight. *Better than by mug shot*, he tried to tell himself, but the joke did little to dampen the anxious hum in his stomach. "Chief's waiting for you with someone from the county sheriff's office."

The news amplified the hum into a low roar. *That has to mean a break in the case*, he thought as he walked over and knocked on the door with Police Chief Craig Perkins painted on the glass.

"You remember Deputy Vincent from the sheriff's office?" Craig asked as he motioned Jake into the room where another man sat in one of two guest chairs in front of the chief's desk.

"Sorta." There had been a parade of law enforcement types those first days after Nat and Kurt died, and most of them were a blur in Jake's memory. "What's up?" Jake asked as he sat down. "Got news?"

"Sorta," Craig said, using Jake's word with a touch of a smile.

Jake felt his stomach drop as he sat down. Was this the moment he'd learn his sister's killer? It still sent him reeling to use that word, but it fit, didn't it? Everyone used the kinder term *accident*, but she and Kurt had been *killed*. The way he saw it, a random shooting was still a murder.

Seeing his face, the chief raised his hand, palm out in a gesture of restraint. "Before you get all riled up, we don't have a suspect yet."

As much as he was dreading concrete news, the idea that they'd *still* not found the guy burned Jake just as fiercely. "Why am I here, then?" he asked a little too loudly.

"Because we think we have the weapon," said the man in a shirt just as dark as Chief Perkins's but with a different badge.

Somehow knowing the physical weapon had been found shoved the whole reality of it into sharper focus. A wave of something like a fever washed over Jake, and he had to remind himself to keep breathing. "If you've got the gun, can't you just trace it back to the guy?"

Perkins gave a *let's be patient* sigh. "It's not that easy in this case."

Jake really wished Chief Perkins would stop saying that particular sentence to him. It shouldn't be hard to find this guy. He shouldn't be able to get away with the horrible thing he'd done. The lives he'd destroyed. "Why's that?"

"The hunting rifle was found four miles away in a wooded area. It's been out in the open for a while—in the rain and such—so any prints are long gone. It registers as stolen, which isn't a big surprise. We're waiting on the ballistics report, but the type matches the bullets lodged in your sister's car."

Hunting rifle. The words made it all sound so much more sinister.

"It does confirm our theory that it was the car the shooter was aiming at, not your sister or her husband specifically. This isn't the sort of firearm you'd use for that. I believe this was just the available weapon, not anything well planned."

The officer's clean, clinical tone made Jake nuts, and his fingers tightened into fists against the office chair's vinyl arms. "Is that supposed to make me feel better? That my sister was murdered *on a whim*?"

"Jake…" Perkins started to rise out of his chair.

"It means," the deputy cut in, turning to face Jake directly, "that it makes it harder to connect a suspect to the crime. We've got no clear motive connecting him or her to your sister or brother-in-law. The weapon, if it matches, is a big step forward."

Jake could hear the unspoken word at the end of that pronouncement. "But…"

"But it means, son, that you might want to prepare yourself for the possibility that we may never know who did this." Perkins's eyes were cautious and apologetic, but that made little difference.

"That's not okay," Jake growled out. "That's not even close to okay."

"I get that," the chief agreed. "And you have my word that both departments will do everything we can to make sure that's not how this turns out. I wish we solved every case, but I hope you know I especially want to solve this

one. You need closure, Sarah needs it, and so does little Cole."

Closure was a soft and cozy term. Jake wanted justice. He craved hard, sharp, full-blown retribution in a
way that scared even him a bit. He had no intention of
living with some vague cloud of not knowing that would
hang over his head the rest of his days. Of Cole's days. It
would be hard to know who had done this—Jake knew
that—but it would be far worse to never know.

"I know it's not what you want, but we wanted to share
what news we had," Deputy Vincent said. "This isn't on
the back burner by any means. It's a priority case for us."

The assurance should have helped, but it didn't. Nat
and Kurt were still gone, and no one knew who had done
it. "What's next?"

"We'll continue our search of the area, start trying
to build a profile of who might do something like this.
Check the known channels for stolen firearms or incidents
with a minivan like your sister's." The deputy steepled
his hands. "We're probably looking at someone with an
issue of some kind—mental illness, addiction, that sort
of thing. But the truth is we just don't know enough to
draw any straight lines to leads yet."

"And I'm sorry about that," Chief Perkins added.
"Truly, I am. It's a terrible loss." He pulled a desk drawer
open. "And while I know it's not much, the guys on the
force pitched in to help you get some of Cole's Christmas
presents." He handed Jake an envelope. "We all felt like
we ought to do something for the poor guy."

Gratitude should be the right response, but it loomed
out of Jake's reach. A mountain of toys under the tree
wouldn't make this Christmas okay. This Christmas had
no hope of being okay. He forced the words "Thank you"

out of his mouth as he took the envelope, ashamed of how insincere they must sound. He thought of what Emma might say, and managed to add, "That's very kind of you."

"If there's anything else we can do, you know we will," Perkins assured him as he rose from his chair.

Jake said the only thing churning in his chest as he rose as well. "Find him. That's what you can do. Find the guy who did this and make him pay." Not exactly turning the other cheek, but it was all Jake had to offer at the moment. God was going to have a lot of work to do on his sorry soul if he was ever going to make it through this whole mess.

A week later, as December began, Emma found herself conducting a costume fitting for the striped Joseph robe on Wyatt Walker.

"Why do I think my brother planned for me to play understudy all along?" The man didn't look particularly happy to be stepping into his older brother's robes for the living nativity. "I'm not exactly leading man material, and he's a real-life new dad," Wyatt said from inside the fabric as he yanked the robe over his tall body.

Emma could only smile. Wyatt's baby nephew Henry showing up two weeks late was the happiest problem she had to solve with the manger scene. "I think Chaz is smart to step out now. Henry's a newborn. There's a lot to deal with when you're a first-time parent."

Wyatt's head appeared from under the yards of biblical-looking robe. "I don't get it. Aren't he and Yvonne a ready-made Mary, Joseph and Baby Jesus?"

The man's naive question showed that Wyatt's new status as the stepfather of twin elementary school girls hadn't taught him everything about parenting. She offered a gentle scowl as she began to measure how much the robe would need to be shortened from the measurements she'd taken of Wyatt's taller brother. "You cannot keep a month-old baby out in the Colorado winter."

"So now it's me who gets to freeze instead of Chaz, while he gets to stay home counting little fingers and toes."

Emma stretched out her arms, cuing Wyatt to do the same. "Yvonne needs Chaz home with her and Henry. I've no doubt your brother playing Joseph was Pauline's idea anyway, not Chaz's."

"Wait…so you're in charge but you didn't pick who plays what part? I half agreed to this nonsense because I thought you chose Margie and Maddie to play angels and I figured I owed you."

"If you owe anyone, it's Norma Binton and the worship committee." Emma twirled her fingers, indicating for Wyatt to turn around.

"So that explains why Carrie Binton is Mary."

Once again, Norma Binton had waged an all-out campaign to get her niece in a prominent position. She'd won and gotten Carrie cast as Mary, and clearly taken that as encouragement to step up her efforts to slide the woman into the preschool director's position. Emma was trying to like Carrie, but it was getting harder.

"I wasn't consulted on casting," she said neutrally as she pinned the back hem of the robe. "All done. You should have plenty of room for a couple of layers under here to stay warm." When Wyatt turned back to face her, she asked, "I take it you know how to hold a baby?"

The question clearly caught him up short, and he mimed a cradling position. "In your arms?"

Get Up To 4 Free Books!

Dear Reader,

IT'S A FACT: if you answer 4 quick questions, we'll send you 4 FREE REWARDS from each series you try!

Try **Love Inspired® Romance Larger-Print** books and fall in love with inspirational romances that take you on an uplifting journey of faith, forgiveness and hope.

Try **Love Inspired® Suspense Larger-Print** books where courage and optimism unite in stories of faith and love in the face of danger.

Or **TRY BOTH!**

I'm not kidding you. As a leading publisher of women's fiction, we value your opinions... and your time. That's why we are prepared to reward you handsomely for completing our mini-survey. In fact, we have 4 Free Rewards for you, including 2 free books and 2 free gifts from each series you try!

Thank you for participating in our survey,

Pam Powers

To get your 4 FREE REWARDS:
Complete the survey below and return the insert today to receive up to 4 FREE BOOKS and FREE GIFTS guaranteed!

"4 for 4" MINI-SURVEY

1 Is reading one of your favorite hobbies?
☐ YES   ☐ NO

2 Do you prefer to read instead of watch TV?
☐ YES   ☐ NO

3 Do you read newspapers and magazines?
☐ YES   ☐ NO

4 Do you enjoy trying new book series with FREE BOOKS?
☐ YES   ☐ NO

Please send me my Free Rewards, consisting of **2 Free Books from each series I select** and **Free Mystery Gifts**. I understand that I am under no obligation to buy anything, as explained on the back of this card.

☐ **Love Inspired® Romance Larger-Print** (122/322 IDL GQ5X)
☐ **Love Inspired® Suspense Larger-Print** (107/307 IDL GQ5X)
☐ **Try Both** (122/322 & 107/307 IDL GQ6A)

FIRST NAME	LAST NAME

ADDRESS

APT.#	CITY

STATE/PROV.	ZIP/POSTAL CODE

EMAIL ☐ Please check this box if you would like to receive newsletters and promotional emails from Harlequin Enterprises ULC and its affiliates. You can unsubscribe anytime.

LI/SLI-520-MS20

"Not like a football. Supporting the head."

Wyatt looked a bit stumped, as if it had not occurred to him baby holding was an actual skill. "Maybe get a little practice with Henry," she suggested. "And I'll tell Carrie to do most of the holding or stick to the manger if little Logan is kind enough to sleep." She began helping Wyatt out of the long robe…until it caught on his belt buckle and promptly split one side seam. Another thirty minutes of mending tagged itself onto the end of Emma's very long task list.

"Oops, sorry," Wyatt said. "See what I mean? I'm not cut out for this. Becky and Art should rethink loaning baby Logan to the likes of me for even one night."

Emma took the robe from him. "Uncle Wyatt's going to have to master it sometime," she replied. "Your twins are going to want to spend lots of time with their new baby cousin."

Wyatt rolled his eyes. "Tell me about it. Mari has taken the girls Henry shopping three times already. Bought him a teddy bear bigger than he is." He pulled his jacket back on. "Are Chaz and Dad still good for the pair of cows? They're not bailing on that, too?"

"Of the very calm variety, please. No horns. With Hank there to supervise." Pauline—who was married to Hank—had promised as much, but Emma felt she ought to confirm it. True to Jake's prediction, no one considered her idea of life-size cutouts to be acceptable with so many ranchers and so much livestock readily available. Jake's fence had better live up to its reputation.

Jake's fence was one of the plans that were supposed to be on her desk yesterday. The library plans had shown up two days late, as well. It was only two and a half weeks before the nativity was to take place, on the Sunday night

before Christmas. Things were starting to look like they'd
be anything but peaceful and calm.

"Hey, I heard about the idea for Cole Wilson," Wyatt
said as he turned to leave the church classroom that had
been temporarily turned into Emma's crèche workroom.
"Brilliant on Pastor Newton's part. Has he told Cole yet?"

"They're waiting until a little closer to the night so
he doesn't get nervous. Or he doesn't end up 'practic-
ing' on pots and pans and trying Jake's patience." Making Cole the little drummer boy was indeed an inspired
idea. Of all the last-minute tasks on her list, whipping
up one more costume so Cole could participate was the
easiest one of all.

Wyatt shook his head. "Probably good for the little
guy to have something fun to look forward to. Tough
business, that. How is he, you think?"

Emma piled the torn robe into a basket. "I can't help
but think all the prayers are working. Jake tells me he
still has nightmares, and he gets a little lost when he's
not quite awake and can't remember why his mom and
dad aren't there. But considering all he's dealing with, I
think he's doing okay."

"I'm sure you're a big part of that," Wyatt offered.
"Don't you listen for a second to what those old hens
are saying."

Emma froze. "Which old hens saying what?"

Hens was plural. Was someone other than Norma Binton wagging tongues about her?

"Pay 'em no mind, like I said. You should get to spend
Thanksgiving wherever you want. That's what I say."

It had been a last-minute invite when Celia's parents
got sick. Were people watching Bo Carter's driveway

or something? Emma walked over to Wyatt. "What are they saying?"

"Hey, look, Jake's a nice enough guy and he sure needs your help. If there's anything going on, that's your business. Wander watches way too much, if you ask me."

"*What* are they saying?" Emma repeated with insistence.

Wyatt huffed and shifted his weight. "Someone saw you in the woods with Jake. On Thanksgiving Day. Not as if it's any of their business, like I said."

Who on earth had been peering into the woods that day? She hadn't seen another soul anywhere among the trees that afternoon. Still, Emma's mind looked back with a sinking feeling to the hug she'd known was a mistake. She was smart enough to know teachers always have to be careful about such things. Perception was everything in some cases, and people jumped to conclusions in a heartbeat in a small town like Wander. She fought the urge to whack her forehead for giving in to his charm for even that careless minute. Her attraction to Jake was better left ignored, unless she wanted to sink her chances at the director position.

"I mean it, Emma," Wyatt urged. "Don't let them tell you what to do."

This was just the kind of thing Norma would pounce on. Had Zosia heard anything? Could Zosia's support shore her up against a gossip fest if things got out of hand? Emma gritted her teeth. It was more important than ever that her abilities shine in the crèche and the library projects now. She couldn't—and wouldn't—back out of helping with Cole, but she was going to have to double down on her vigilance against anything that might look improper with Jake.

Chapter Ten

Some days Jake loved his job. Today was not one of them. Everything that could go wrong had gone wrong, and his patience was falling way short of demand these days. Construction was a Plan B business as Bo liked to say, meaning that things went wrong all the time and a builder's true skill was how he pivoted to cope.

Jake wasn't on Plan B, he was on D, E, F and maybe down toward X, Y and Z. Part of it was his own fault—he hadn't been able to get last week's news about how they might never know who fired the shots from that overpass out of his head. The injustice of it seemed to be eating at him in ways that couldn't be healthy. He'd forgotten an appointment, messed up two orders at the hardware store and misplaced a vital set of blueprints in the last week alone.

Telling Emma he had all the materials for the stable was looking like it would be today's only victory. Jake parked his truck in the house garage, taking a moment and a few deep breaths to try to wipe away the day's frustration before he greeted Cole. How had Natalie managed to keep the hopeful, caring expression she always wore?

"He's got you, and that will make all the difference," Emma kept saying. But was that really enough? Caring for a five-year-old was feeling like an endless uphill climb, even with Emma's huge help. Jake thought about Cole's wide eyes, his wild hugs and his priceless giggles. That was what mattered, not uneaten vegetables or late bedtimes or tantrums. Sarah said she expected to be back on her feet by January—he just had to hang on until then.

Grabbing his workbag and commanding his attitude to improve, Jake pushed open the door that led from the garage into the kitchen. "Hi, honey, I'm home!" he called as a joke.

Emma glared at him. A sharp, hard glare that slowed his steps. "Okay, maybe not so funny," he said as he cautiously laid his bag on the counter. Maybe her day hadn't gone any better than his.

"Not funny at all." Emma's words were short and soft. "Cole is next door playing with their dog so we can have a conversation."

"A conversation" sounded way more like "I'm about to lay into you about something." Maybe ice cream on waffles wasn't everyone's idea of a nutritious breakfast, but this morning Jake had felt it a victory to have gotten Cole to eat anything at all. Still, even that shortcoming didn't seem to merit the scowl she was giving him.

"Okay," he said slowly, walking around the counter stools and into the kitchen as if land mines were hidden beneath the floor tiles.

"There will be no hugging. Ever again. No touching, no jokes, no friendly contact of any kind between us. Am I clear?"

So now would definitely not be the time to say how the memory of her in his arms was distracting him as much as the injustice of Nat's unsolved case. Jake's fascination with Emma was kicking into a surprising overdrive— despite the fact that she wasn't at all his usual type. He truly enjoyed coming home to the warmth she brought to the house and to Cole. He found himself compiling a daily list of things he wanted to share with her—small stories, little observations, each tiny win against the wave of sorrow that still stalked him.

After Thanksgiving, he'd started to believe she felt the same. Emma's current expression, however, left no doubt that he'd been wrong.

"Want to tell me what brought this on?"

When her eyebrows furrowed together, Jake wished he'd phrased that differently. His conversational skills fell short when blindsided by an angry woman, it seemed.

"People are talking." Her declaration made it sound as if that should explain everything.

It didn't. "About what?"

She cocked her head to one side, chin jutting out in annoyance. "About us."

"About how you're saving my life by helping out with Cole?" That made her look like a hero in his book, not the angry cat currently staring him down.

"About how we hugged in the woods behind Bo and Toni's house." She nearly hissed it, as if they'd been caught under the high school bleachers. Some days Wander Canyon's ability to stick its collective nose into other people's business made him want to snarl.

"Who on earth saw that? I was just being nice to you, for crying out loud. So now I can't be nice to people?" It was, of course, a bit more than just *nice* from where he sat, but he wasn't going to say that now.

"*You* can't be *that nice* to *me*." She pointed at him with each of the emphasized words. When he stared at her, still blindsided, she added, "People are…" Her pointing dissolved into a vague wave of her hand, as if the words were unspeakable.

"You mean…people are pairing us off? Who jumped to that ridiculous conclusion?" He shouldn't have used that word. It wasn't ridiculous. After all, in his thoughts *he was* starting to pair them off.

"I don't know who. But I can't have this. Especially not now." She looked around the kitchen as if the very house had spread the information. "I should never have let Pastor Newton talk me into this."

Something sank in Jake's chest. He'd rather liked the idea that Emma had gladly taken it upon herself to help him with Cole. That Pastor Newton had pressured her to step in bugged him in any number of ways. At the very least, it felt like yet another vote for people thinking him unable to care for Cole properly.

Which led to a different fear. "You're not quitting on me, are you?" He should have stopped himself before saying, "I can't pull this off without you," but he didn't. After all, it was true. He and Cole needed Emma. Her guidance and encouragement were their best defense against the grief and dread Jake felt as if he fought back every single day.

"Of course not," she replied. Jake was grateful her expression told him she found the idea unthinkable. "The last thing Cole needs is anyone else abandoning him."

So this was about Cole. Some part of Jake wanted it to be even a tiny bit about him, but it was Cole who really mattered here. Cole's long-term happiness was way more important than how much Jake enjoyed Emma's company.

"I'm glad to hear it," he said. When that felt a little too needy, Jake added, "I hate the idea of those gossipy old hens winning on this."

The friction that had bristled between them from the moment he walked in began to settle down. She leaned against the opposite counter, the hard set of her shoulders softening. "The director's job is important to me. Cole's well-being is important to me. I don't want one to come at the cost of the other."

"It should never have to." Whoever had been lurking—spying—in those woods just added themselves to Jake's list of unknown culprits he'd like to see get what was coming to them. He didn't much like the size of his appetite for revenge lately, and this wasn't helping. Jake took a long, slow inhale and unclenched his fingers. His tactic had always been to defiantly ignore things like this, but Emma didn't have that luxury. "Tell me what you want me to do."

"No more socializing. No staying for burgers or anything like that."

He'd been afraid she was going to say something like that. He'd begun to think of more ways to do social things with her, and so had Cole. "We might have a problem with that."

"Why?" She crossed her arms over her chest, defenses rising again.

Jake shifted his weight. "The Sunday School friends party? The one where the kids get to invite someone for hot chocolate and caroling?"

"I know about it."

"Cole told me last night he wants you to be his invited friend."

Her hands lowered. "Shouldn't that be you?"

"Well, no. Every kid gets parents and a special friend.

Plan B was going to be Grandma Sarah and me, but since we're on Plan C… I have to play parental stand-in while you have been granted special friend status." He reached into the kitchen drawer beside him and produced the sweet little invitation Cole had made in Sunday School earlier. He handed it to her, face up so she could see *Miss Emma* written on it in Cole's still-clumsy lettering.

All the edge went out of her eyes as she held the red construction paper, Christmas bell adorned with globs of glitter.

"It's not a preschool function, which plants it squarely in the social realm. But, Emma," he added, catching her eye, "I haven't got the heart to make him do Plan D. Do you?"

"No," she said quietly.

The following Thursday evening, Emma pulled the door to her house shut and leaned against it with a weary sigh. She understood why they'd moved the preschool board meeting up a week on account of the holiday, but it just felt like piling more onto an already growing workload. Each of the week's three school days had felt like endless struggles. December tenth, the day of her mother's death, had come yesterday and left a swath of sadness in its wake. Christmas was now just two weeks away, and the children's attention spans were fast dissolving while their wiggly energy had begun to jack up. The coming week would be worse, getting progressively crazier as the holiday drew near. Every preschool teacher dreaded the week before Christmas.

I can do this, she told herself. After all, the nativity plans were on schedule. All the costumes had been constructed, and fittings—and in one case, rippings—were well under way. Even a good menagerie of animals had been secured. She would pull this off, if Jake could be counted on to have the set finished in time.

She'd be lying if she said the prospect of her success hinging on Jake didn't worry her a bit. After all, the library was far behind schedule. Still, the only person putting any urgency on that project was Jake himself. And perhaps Norma, who seemed eager—if not pleased—to watch the responsibilities pile on Emma's plate. *I can handle it. I'm tougher than you know, Norma Binton.*

But what if it was more than Norma? Hadn't Wyatt spoken as if there were multiple people gossiping about her? She'd been cautious recently, but that fear was enough to make her slump against her door tonight. The thought of someone peering through the trees at what she'd considered a private moment between herself and Jake made her stomach burn. She and Jake had been meticulous about keeping a wide professional margin between them. Even so, Emma hated how the worry over public scrutiny had made her glance around the church service and wonder each of the past two Sundays. Who had been in the woods? Who was gossiping and spreading their disapproval of something they couldn't hope to understand? It had been two weeks since Thanksgiving, but no one had yet said anything directly to her about it. Had the incident blown over, or was it festering under the surface?

She had found Wander to be such a welcoming place. It touched her how the community had risen to help Sarah and then Jake. The way that interconnectedness had now turned on her felt like fast and mean whiplash. They didn't know how hard these holidays were for her, how she was fighting this terrible sense of something looming.

They don't know because you haven't told them, Emma lectured herself. She hadn't even told Zosia or Pastor Newton. It was her own fault no one knew why she and Jake shared grief and sorrow over this holiday. She'd chosen not to tell anyone about her family's tragic past and its sad present. *Do you really think that would have made any difference?* she argued with herself. *The Normas of this world look for faults to crack open, hunt for fights to pick.*

Emma tried to give herself a pep talk as she tossed her mail on the kitchen counter. *Don't let them get to you.* The bright white of a postcard stilled her hands as she picked through the envelopes.

Sam.

Her eye went to the postmark, smudged but readable. It was from six days ago, from a small town two hours from here. That should mean something, but she'd already failed to make out any kind of direction or sense from the scattering of locations. The drawing was a bare stretch of highway fading off into the mountains. Scraggly trees lined one side of the road while a broad red line ran down the other. A stream? Some imaginary border in Sam's tangled mind? While the drawing was simpler than the others, it somehow seemed angrier.

Emma sat down at her table, clutching the card in both hands. Was Sam trying to tell her something? Reach out? What did the red mean, if anything? Did he not realize he'd given her no way to communicate with him?

Her breath hitched as Emma realized there was one difference with this card. He had signed it. Down in one corner, at the end of the broad red line, he'd scrawled— *SAM*. His handwriting wasn't much better than Cole's, and never had been despite how well he could draw.

That signature had to mean something. He'd never bothered to sign a card before. Did it mean he was getting better, feeling steadier? Or was it a sign of things getting worse?

Lost for what else to do, Emma closed her eyes in prayer. *I don't know if Sam believes in You—or ever did— but I know he is still Your child. This feels too large for me. He's lost in every way possible. I'll admit it because You already know: I'm afraid to help him. I'm afraid to let him back into my life. He's been nothing but damage and chaos, and I'm just starting to feel settled. I don't even know what to pray for here, so maybe I'll just stick with Thy Will Be Done.*

She wanted to feel better or settled or at least more at peace, but no such comfort came. When she opened her eyes, her gaze landed on the little nativity scene she'd bought at an art fair last year arranged in the kitchen bay window for lack of a fireplace mantel in her little house. Between her and Jake, they'd managed to get a fair amount of the decorations up at Cole's home. No tree yet, but at least it looked festive. It had felt good to make Cole's Christmas happen, even if it did make her own home feel sparse—lacking in family, in contrast to the flurry of family-focused activities and sentiments all around.

Even if I found the strength to reach out to Sam, she added to her previous prayer, *I haven't got a way. If You send one, will You also send the strength?*

Emma didn't know the answer. She didn't even know if she wanted an answer to such a risky thought. Her new life here in Wander Canyon seemed to be balanced on a shaky edge, ready to tumble should anything go wrong.

All the stress was getting to her—she hadn't felt well all day.

She ought to call Zosia. Or Pastor Newton. It made so little sense not to let them know her struggles with Sam. But telling them would mean admitting the distance she'd forced between herself and her family, and she couldn't bring herself to do that just yet. Maybe she could go to them after she'd made it through this holiday mess and she'd either been given the director position or it had gone to someone else.

Emma almost ignored her cell phone when it went off, until she noticed it was Zosia. Divine timing? She wasn't at all sure when she hit the button to accept the call and said, "Hi, Zosia."

"We've got a problem," Zosia said without any more greeting than that. "I've gotten five calls from moms whose kids are down with flu symptoms."

Emma instinctively put her hand to her forehead, jumping to conclusions about how she hadn't felt well today. She'd thought the warmth and irritability were just symptoms of stress.

"How are you feeling?" Zosia asked.

Lost, worried, scrutinized and possibly infected, Emma thought. For all her efforts to guard against infection from Celia's family, the bug had found her anyway. "Not so great, now that you mention it."

"That's it," Zosia declared. "We're shutting down tomorrow to disinfect the classroom. The last thing we need is a Christmas plague on our hands."

Today had gone wrong on so many levels; this felt like the last straw. "Who do you need me to call?" She tried to keep the frustrated tears that threatened out of her voice.

Zosia heard them anyway. "Oh, *kochanie*, no one. Stay

home tomorrow." Emma had heard Zosia use the Polish endearment when children skinned their knees. "I can make the calls, and I'll grab the church janitorial staff and a few board members and we'll take care of it. Don't you come in." After a pause, she added, "What do you need? Have you got supplies to hunker down?"

Every preschool teacher worth her salt was always prepared for germ warfare. She walked over to her pantry, grateful to see two bottles of ginger ale, three cans of soup and a box of crackers all waiting to intervene. "I'm fine. Actually, I think a solid night's sleep is all I'll need." Despite her preparedness, the bag filled with unfinished costume alterations still mocked her from where she'd dropped it by the door.

"I'll call Jake," she said, knowing her possible illness had multiple consequences for him. Poor Jake was about to learn the bane of every working parent's existence: sick days. And she knew he was already far behind on multiple fronts. "He'll have to call in to work, I expect."

"Him and a bunch of other parents," Zosia commiserated. "'Tis the season. I'll check in with you midmorning tomorrow to make sure you're okay. Go to bed. Now."

Despite it being dinnertime, Emma was growing too queasy to do anything but comply. She walked to her bathroom and plucked the bottle of Tylenol from the medicine cabinet shelf. "Will do."

Cole. Sam. Norma. Jake. Nativities, libraries and the flu. Was there a medicine bottle big enough to do battle with all the knots in her life at the moment?

Emma took two Tylenol, donned her coziest pajamas, grabbed a box of tissues and the big plush throw off her bed, and headed back to mount her defense from the living room couch. She'd give the medicine half an hour to kick in and give Jake the bad news then.

Chapter Eleven

Emma would probably have six reasons why Jake shouldn't be pounding on her door at eight thirty on a Friday morning, but she hadn't shown up at the house and hadn't answered her phone. Cole was in the back seat of his truck, and Emma's car was still in her driveway. Not even Norma Binton could call an early morning wellness check "social."

He rang the bell. "Emma?" he called. No answer.

He tried to look in the window, but the drapes were pulled. Jake went back and banged on the door. "Emma!"

When no answer came, Jake looked back at Cole in his truck, wondering if it had been a smart move to bring the boy. Should a five-year-old watch his uncle break down a door? Should he see whatever crisis might be lurking on the other side?

He was raising his hand to bang again when the door slowly opened, revealing a mottled face that looked somewhat like Emma's on the other side. She'd probably have *twelve* reasons why he shouldn't be there now, but none of that mattered. "Are you okay?"

That was a pretty foolish question based on her current appearance. Half her hair was up in some kind of elastic while the other half stuck out in all directions. Her face was blotchy and flushed as she winced at the bright morning sunshine coming in from behind him. She was still absolutely adorable—although Jake was sure she'd never agree. "You are not okay," he answered for her, pushing the door farther open.

"Don't come in," she cautioned, wobbling a bit as she did so. "I'm contagious."

"I think that horse already left the barn," he said, reaching out to her with one hand as he waved Cole in with the other. She looked like she might fall over any second. "Does school know?"

Her bleary eyes widened. "I was supposed to call you last night. Loads of kids are sick so they canceled to wipe down the classroom today."

So no school, and no Emma. Today had officially blown itself to pieces and it wasn't even nine o'clock. "Let me in?" He wasn't going to let her refuse, but thought it kinder to phrase it as a question.

"You look gross," came Cole's frank assessment from beside Jake.

"I feel awful. I…" Her mouth clamped shut, and without another word, she rushed off in what Jake could only guess was the direction of her bathroom.

"Ewww…" Cole said as he peered after her.

"Sometimes things get ewwy," Jake said, walking farther into the room. Normally he wasn't the caretaker type, but this was Emma, and she was alone. "If we don't have to worry about getting you to school today, we might as well make ourselves useful here."

Jake looked about the room to see the evidence of a usually tidy Emma's rough night. A circle of crumpled tissues surrounded one corner of the couch like a mushroom ring, several blankets were piled up in pastel mounds and two pairs of socks lay on the floor. On the coffee table stood a collection of empty glasses, three open sleeves of crackers and a bottle of Tylenol tipped over on its side. As much as he loved his bachelorhood, he knew one of the worst parts of a single life was being sick solo. He would help her, but he wasn't exactly sure how. With a pang, he remembered that Natalie would have been his first call for advice in this situation. *You're on your own, bub, improvise.*

As he was formulating a plan, Emma emerged from the bathroom, leaning against the wall as she walked. "Don't stay," she started to argue.

"Don't argue," he countered. He was going to be her champion against this onslaught of germs. After all, she'd done so much for him. "Feel well enough to take a shower?"

"Maybe," she ventured. "Why?"

"'Cuz you look gross," Cole repeated without any hint of awareness that it was a rude thing to say.

Jake shot Cole a look. Emma tried to laugh, but it dissolved into a weak cough. "I expect I do," she managed with more grace than Jake thought he would have shown under the circumstances. She really was one of the kindest souls he'd ever met. And still a rumpled, wobbly sort of adorable that made helping her irresistible…even with the "gross" factor.

"You clean up you," Jake offered, "and we'll take care of out here."

"But…"

"Nope. We're not leaving. End of discussion." He tried

to emulate Natalie's *do as you're told* face as he pointed Emma back down the hall.

After a moment of hesitation, Emma realized she had no choice. "Thanks," she said as she turned.

Jake surveyed the disaster zone as he and Cole took off their jackets and hung them by the door. Walking into the kitchen revealed more mess, but gave him an idea. Checking under the sink and in one drawer, he located a trash bag and a pair of salad tongs. Handing them to Cole, he instructed, "Use these to pick up all the tissues and any other trash. No touching with your hands. Got it?"

Convinced this sounded enough like a game, Cole started toward the living room with his new implements until Jake had another idea. Waving his nephew back, he retrieved a pair of pink flowered rubber gloves from next to Emma's sink as an extra precaution. "Wear these, too." He cuffed them up until they fit floppily onto Cole's small hands. The whole getup was so silly he almost pulled out his cell phone and snapped a picture, but decided against it.

As Cole went to mount his tiny attack against the tissues, Jake started in on the kitchen. As he loaded the dishwasher, he racked his brain about who to call for further help. Settling on Toni, he called Bo's cell and set it on the counter on speakerphone as he filled the sink with hot soapy water. Jake Sanders, heroic soldier of domestic disinfection—who would believe this if they saw it?

"Is Toni home?" he asked when Bo answered.

"She's at the shop already getting more stuff ready for Christmas. Where are you?"

Jake was grateful Bo didn't immediately ask, "Why aren't you here yet?" even though it was a valid question.

"I went to Emma's when she didn't show up and didn't

answer her phone. She's pretty sick. I need female coping strategies." He left out the silent *and I can't call Nat*, which his brain finished the sentence with. "Preschool is closed so I've got Cole. I'll be in as soon as I can figure out how to make this all work."

"Take your time," Bo answered, even though Jake knew he was throwing a monster of a wrench into their already busy day. "I got this."

Thank You for friends like Bo, Jake prayed as he clicked off the call, looked up the number for Redding's General Store and dialed.

"Merry Christmas from Redding's," Toni answered in a cheerful voice.

"Merry Christmas from preschool flu patient zero's house," he said, trying to sound equally cheerful. "It's Jake. I'm at Emma's and she's pretty sick. What do I need to do?"

"Does she need to see a doctor?"

He hadn't even thought about that. Hearing that the shower hadn't started, he called, "Do you need a doctor, Emma?" down the hall. He ignored the moan Toni gave him from the other end of the line.

"No!" came the reply from Emma, punctuated by several sorry-sounding coughs.

"She says no," he reported back.

"Do you believe her?"

It hadn't occurred to him not to, but it sounded exactly like something Nat would have said. "I think so. This just looks like garden-variety flu. Miserable but not lethal."

"I'll give you a list for Caldwell's. They'll deliver."

A drugstore that delivered was one of the great blessings of a town like Wander Canyon even before the rest of the world caught on. He couldn't decide if it was a plus or a minus that Norma Binton worked behind the counter, but that couldn't matter at the moment. Grabbing a pen, he rifled through the mail on Emma's table looking for a scrap to write on. His eyes stopped for a moment at an odd, hand-drawn postcard amongst the usual collection of bills and store flyers, noting for a split second that it had the signature *SAM* on it. Wasn't that her brother's name? Didn't she say they weren't in contact?

He didn't have time to ponder that. "Okay, shoot," he told Toni, and wrote down the list of medicines and supplies she ticked off. "Hey, thanks," he said when she was done. Swallowing a bit hard, he added, "I'm short my usual source for these kinds of things." It seemed like every situation offered up a new reason to miss Natalie lately.

"I know," Toni said warmly. "But you've got others ready to help. And you're sweet to step in for Emma. Do you want me to call Zosia at the school?"

"No, I think that's covered."

"Keep me posted. I might be able to swing by later in the afternoon. Or send Bo or Mari if we're too busy."

Jake wasn't sure the mother of twin girls would appreciate an invitation to the germ festival right before Christmas, but he said thanks anyway as he ended the call.

Cole returned to the kitchen, his garbage bag filled with tissues. "Got 'em all!" he declared with pride.

"Awesome job, kiddo." He fished a tub of disinfectant wipes he'd seen under the sink on a suggestion from Toni. "While you've got that battle gear on, wipe down the table and any counters you can reach."

"Yes, sir!" Cole said, saluting Jake with a floppy flowered hand that made Jake smile.

As he heard the shower start, Jake finished loading

the dishwasher and dumped the remnants of a half-eaten pot of soup down the garbage disposal. An absurd satisfaction glowed in his stomach at being able to rescue Emma. She was always so pulled together that the sight of her undone and a bit helpless buried itself in a corner of his heart and refused to leave.

He countered that sentiment by remembering how ticked off Emma would probably be as soon as she recovered. After all, Wander was always watching, and his truck was in her driveway before nine in the morning.

Who cares? But that wasn't fair. He knew she had to worry about her reputation. And that was mean old Norma Binton's fault.

If Old Biddy Binton should happen to answer Caldwell's phone this morning, he might be tempted to give the judgmental old hen a piece of his mind.

She didn't. So Jake simply gave the list to Dan Caldwell, the pharmacist, told him to put it on his account and deliver it to Emma's address, and sat down to wait for it to all arrive.

It took the entire weekend for Emma to recover, but by the following Wednesday things had settled back down to normal. Emma opted to bring some specially made cookies to church that she'd ordered for Cole from the Wander Bakery. She wondered if anyone would believe the way Jake had taken such tender care of her last Friday morning. The practical side of him had outfitted her with more Tylenol, two more cans of soup and one of those hot-drink flu medicines from the drugstore. The look on his face as he tucked her into a corner of the couch, spreading a freshly washed afghan over her, had made her want to reach for his hand. Her instincts had been right—there was a first-class softy hiding under that hardened bachelor exterior. No simple thank-you would do in this case.

Emma had decided to ask permission to be the one to tell Cole he'd be given the role of the little drummer boy. She knew it would mean as much to Jake as it did to Cole—maybe even more. Hoping to make it as big a deal as possible, Emma had asked the bakery to make a dozen cookies decorated like drums. Jake had mentioned he would be working on the nativity stable in the church basement that afternoon, so she could deliver the news and the goodies there without having to make a "social" visit to his house.

She found the pair hard at work, Cole sitting among an assortment of screws and nails and several small jars while Jake nailed together the stable frame.

"You better?" Cole asked. His question was as bright as the smile Jake gave her when she walked into the section of the church's lower level that had been cleared for storage and construction of the nativity. Did that man know how disarming his smile could be? This was Jake Sanders—of course he did. Still, she was grateful for the genuine pleasure in his grin.

"Much better, thank you," Emma replied. "You didn't catch my germs, did you?" She considered that a major blessing, given how much time they spent together. It touched her deeply that Jake had risked infection for both him and Cole, and that he'd done so out of concern for her.

Cole shook his head. "Nope. Uncle Jake says we're boo-poof."

Jake put down the hammer and walked toward Emma. "Bulletproof," Jake corrected. That was Jake, using a brash term she wasn't sure was a wise choice to add to a child's vocabulary. Especially given Cole's circumstances. She chose to let it slide, since Jake had been so kind to her. *Just be glad neither of them caught the bug,* she told herself.

Truth be told, Emma was now far more worried about "catching" something else. Jake looked truly glad to see her, and the gleam in his eyes made an unwelcome warmth rise in her stomach. How many men would do what he'd done for her? His attentions had broken through her lowered defenses, and that unwise feeling growing between them had doubled.

While he'd never come out and said it, his actions that morning had shown her in a dozen ways that he wouldn't mind if things warmed further between them. And that could spell trouble. Knowing Jake's talent for ignoring what people thought, he probably wouldn't see any issue with pursuing it despite her request for caution. He didn't strike her as the compliant type—which was half of what made his rescue mission so heartwarming. She had little doubt that keeping the boundaries drawn between them would clearly fall to her. And that was a challenge, because her thoughts were straying more and more to this handsome uncle and how much she enjoyed the time they spent together.

"I'm glad to see you well underway," she said, hoping to keep the conversation off his recent rescue mission.

"We'll make it," Jake said. "I want you to pull this off with flying colors." He tossed an engaging grin her way. "Or is that flying angels we have heard on high?"

"Are we gonna have flying angels?" Cole asked, impressed.

"We will have three little angels," she replied. "And they'll have sparkly wings, but none of them will be flying." She pointed toward the box of hardware and the collection of small jars. "What are you doing there?" she asked.

"I'm sorting," Cole declared. "Uncle Jake said my hands were the best size to help."

For a man who declared himself clueless about parenting, Emma kept being amazed by the man's resourcefulness with his young charge. That great big heart of his kept peeking out from behind the persona he showed everyone—everyone but her, that is.

Cole's eyes strayed to the bakery box. "Whatcha got?"

"I'm glad you noticed. I've got a special goody and some special news for my two heroes." She immediately regretted using the term, even though she was thankful for what they'd done for her. Emma set the box down on the table and let Cole pull it open by the string.

"Whoa!" he said as he viewed the dozen green and red cookie drums. "Cookies!"

It was fun to make him smile. Given how sad his past weeks had been, every smile felt like a victory of hope. "Not just any cookies, mind you," she teased, unable to wipe the wide smile from her own face. "These are drummer boy cookies."

Jake's eyes widened a bit, but Cole looked baffled. "Huh?"

"These cookies have two jobs," she went on.

"To fill my tummy?" Cole asked.

"Okay," Emma said with a laugh, "three jobs, then. The first is to fill your tummy. And maybe your uncle's, too."

Cole confirmed this task by taking a cookie from the box and indulging in a big bite. "They're good at that job."

"Their second job is to thank you both for being so

nice to me when I was sick. But their third job might be the most special. These cookies are to tell you that you get to play a special role in the nativity scene. You get to be the little drummer boy."

Cole's eyes lit up. "Like the song?"

"Exactly like the song. He gives his special talent to the Baby Jesus to welcome him the night He's born."

"Me?"

Emma almost wished she hadn't caught the radiant glow in Jake's eyes before she answered Cole. "Yep, you. What do you think of that?"

Cole's adorable grin gave her all the answer she needed.

"Whose idea was that?" Jake asked. He was even more touched than she'd expected him to be.

"I'd like to say it was all mine, but it was both Pastor Newton and me together."

Jake cleared his throat. "Well, thanks to both of you. That's great. Isn't it, Cole?"

"I get to be in the manger scene!" Cole declared with endearing pride.

"We wanted to give you a nice big happy memory to keep this Christmas." Emma waited for any signs of sadness to cross the child's face, but he seemed to be able to stay in the happiness of this moment.

"We could use a few of those," Jake agreed.

"I know," she said quietly as Cole gleefully finished off his cookie. She couldn't ever hope to reduce the sadness of this first Christmas without his parents. But doing all she could to give him a few happy memories, too, was within her reach. And Jake's, too, if she could remind him.

"My turtles make me happy," Cole said with his mouth full.

Emma crouched down to the boy's height. "And you see, that's a good thing. When I know I have lots of reasons to feel sad, I try to make a list of all my happy things. I try to see if I can come up with more happy things—even if they are very small—than sad things. Sometimes that's hard, especially when the sad things are very big. But it always makes me feel better."

Cole nodded with a child's quick acceptance, but one glance told Emma that Jake thought that far too simple an answer for the large-scale sorrow they were facing. "It really works," she replied to his doubtful expression.

"I'll have to try it sometime," he said, even though his tone sounded as though he wouldn't.

"I happen to know the drum is upstairs in Pastor Newton's office. Would you like to see it? Maybe he'll let you take it home to practice."

"Sure!" Cole said instantly.

"Why don't you go on upstairs with Miss Emma while I get some of these last bits of wood cut?" Jake suggested.

Emma hoped Jake's idea was more about trying to run the bigger power tools out of the boy's presence than any sour opinion of the amount of drumming about to take place in his household. "Let's go see your drum."

"I might eat a cookie while you're gone," Jake teased. His sense of humor was coming back, and that made her glad.

Cole turned back to his uncle. "Uncle Jake," the boy said, "you can always have some of my cookies."

Jake wasn't the only man in that house with a great big heart.

Chapter Twelve

Jake took the stairs three at a time up toward the pastor's office. He'd been sawing for a few minutes while Cole was upstairs getting his drum when his phone had vibrated. The incoming call was from Chief Perkins at the police department. Perkins's update raised such an urgency in Jake's chest that he knew he had to go over there right now, but he couldn't hope to do that with Cole in tow. If Emma or Pastor Newton wouldn't take Cole for the next hour or so, he'd keep asking until he found someone who could. This had no hope of waiting.

The drumming let him know Cole and Emma were still in Pastor Newton's office. "Hey, guys," he tried to say cheerfully, only it came out sounding strangled. "Can I borrow Emma for a second?"

Pastor Newton and Emma both gave him startled looks, but he couldn't worry about that at the moment. "Of course," Pastor Newton said with an eyebrow raised in silent question. "I can give Cole a few tips." He squatted down on the ground in front of Cole as Emma rose from her chair with a similar look of worry. "Did you know I used to be in a marching band in high school,

Cole?" Pastor Newton asked cheerfully as he watched Jake nearly pull Emma from the room.

Jake ducked into a nearby meeting room and closed the door behind them. "Can you take Cole for an hour or so?"

"I can make a call and move something, yes." She put a hand on his arm. "Jake, what's happened?"

Every second he wasn't heading toward the police station felt like it dragged on. "I just heard from Perkins. They might have a lead."

"What?"

"The highway authority uncovered some video from a traffic study they were doing of that section of highway the week Nat and Kurt were killed." It was the first time the words had left his mouth without his choking on them. "There's some guy. Standing on the overpass watching cars. For three days in a row." That had to be a lead. It had to.

"Do they know who?"

"Not yet. I think he's facing the other way. But it's got to be something or Perkins wouldn't have called me. I need to go over there. Now. Can you take Cole?" The need to see this guy, to put his eyes on the person who might have taken Nat from him, from Cole, felt as if it had set fire to his insides. Still, he had enough sense to know he could not expose Cole to this new development. "Please," he implored.

"Of course," Emma said. "Between Pastor and I, we'll cover it. Unless…do you need him to go over there with you? Are you sure you should do this alone?"

If he was going to be staring at Natalie's killer, he wasn't going to be on his best behavior and might not want the pastor to witness it. "I'm fine. You two cover Cole, that's what I need."

"All right, then. I'll take Cole back to the house. We'll practice drumming and make a Happy List until I hear from you."

If this was the lead Jake thought it was, there wasn't a Happy List in the world long enough to balance this out. Why hadn't God realized yet how ill-equipped he was to take on this sort of thing for someone Cole's age? *Stick around*, he prayed again, not yet ready to ask for peace or calm or any wise spiritual response.

Jake gave Emma's hand a quick squeeze. "Thanks." Without bothering to gather his tools or even clean up the work space in the basement, Jake pushed out the side door of the church and drove the six blocks to the police station at record speed.

Chief Perkins met him at the door. "We don't know if it's a solid lead. I almost didn't call you."

"I want to see it," Jake demanded.

"I've got it in my office," the chief said as he led Jake down the hallway. "It's grainy. It's from a distance. I'm not sure what we'll be able to pull from it."

"Who stalks an overpass unless they're plotting something?" Jake ducked into the office, his pulse clanging in his ears. He wouldn't consider the possibility that this didn't lead to Nat's killer.

Perkins closed the door. "Even if it is the suspect—and I'm not saying that it is, hear me?—that doesn't mean we can identify him from what we see." He glared at Jake. "Don't make me regret showing you this. Get a hold of yourself."

Jake shoved his temper down far enough to show Perkins whatever he needed to see in order to play that video.

"Okay," he said as calmly as he could despite the burning roar persisting in his stomach.

Perkins pressed a few buttons on a laptop and monitor that had been rolled into the room on a cart. A series of three grainy black-and-white video frames came up, each with digital time stamps running across the bottom. Each frame showed the overpass from the same overhead angle, as if the camera was mounted on the highway streetlight just down the road. "Where is he?"

The chief held out a cautionary hand, then pressed another button on the laptop. The first frame kicked into motion, and Jake felt his gut drop as a dark figure walked onto the overpass. Something bone deep and angry inside him told Jake this was Nat's killer. He was staring at the man who stole Cole's parents from him. Who stole his sister from him. Jake realized his fingernails were digging into his palms as he watched the guy just stand there.

"He does that for twenty-eight minutes," Chief Perkins said. "Just stands there."

Jake looked at the chief, biting back the accusation he wanted to shout at the top of his lungs.

"It's not a crime to watch traffic," Perkins warned. He seemed almost reluctant to set the second video in motion. The video was almost the same, with only the weather and a change of clothes to set it apart from the first one. A solitary man came from one end of the screen, walked to the section of the overpass that bridged the highway traffic and stood there for a stretch of time. The third offered no new information, just a repeat of the same actions.

"Is he there the day Nat died?"

"This was a temporary camera set up for a traffic study. It wasn't up the day of Natalie's accident."

Accident. There was that word again. Natalie hadn't died in an accident as far as he was concerned. Kurt and Natalie had been killed. "That's gotta be him," Jake declared.

"This is a *possible* lead," Perkins emphasized. "It places someone at the scene. But that's all. And not on the day in question."

Jake tried to remember every crime show he'd ever watched. "You've got the weapon and the guy at the scene."

The chief halted the video display. "We have a *probable* weapon and an *unknown person* visiting the scene a week earlier. Doing nothing illegal. They could be totally unrelated."

Jake didn't believe it for a single second. This was the guy. He jabbed a finger at the chief. "You don't believe that."

Perkins stared at the screen. "No, I don't. I do think this may be our guy. But none of that changes the fact that this isn't enough to tell us who this man is. Or why he's there. It's a piece of the puzzle, yes. It's progress. I thought I owed you that." He shifted his gaze away from the video monitor to give Jake a stern look. "You gonna make me think twice about showing you this?"

Jake pressed his lips together and told himself to dial it down.

The chief softened his expression. "You've got Cole to think of. I've seen things like this eat people alive. Don't let that happen to you." He planted both hands on his desk and leaned in Jake's direction. "Listen, son. Even if we do find the guy—and I'm determined to see that we do—you're still going to have to make some kind of peace with this eventually."

Jake thought about what Emma had told him. Her father and brother had never put themselves back together after what happened to her mother. And yet she had. So it had to be some kind of choice. Or the grace of God. Or both. She'd found a way through the mess, even when the rest of her family hadn't.

He needed her.

He'd begun to realize that, in a dozen small ways, but it hit him like a shock of cold water just now. He *needed* her. He and Cole were making it because of Emma's encouragement, her gentle spirit and whatever she could teach them about how to make a life past a mess like this. And then there was a deep, insistent pull toward her, way down inside him, that wasn't taking no for an answer. One that had nothing to do with grief or loss or childcare or anything practical—something unfamiliar that itched under his skin and felt like the best light against all the darkness threatening him lately.

Were all the silly gossips in Wander Canyon looking down their noses really going to stand in the way of that? Was there really a rule about Emma seeing him socially because he was now the guardian of a student? Or was that just Norma and her fellow hens passing judgment?

"I'll try to pull it together, Chief," he reassured Perkins. "I want you to feel like you can keep me in the loop without me going all overboard about it." Getting an idea, he asked, "Can you make me a copy of that video, or a printout or something?" Maybe if he looked at it long enough, or showed it to enough people, someone would notice something important.

"I can give you still shots of the clearest frames." Perkins furrowed his eyebrows in concern. "But are you sure you want to have those?"

Of course he wasn't sure. But he'd rather go down that rabbit hole than leave anything undone. "No, but I think it will help."

Emma watched Cole bang his drum around the house and tried to be grateful for the distraction. She looked at the collection of little pictures they'd made together after having a snack, Cole's Happy List. Turtles, a drum, a funny stick drawing of Uncle Jake, chocolate chip cookies and a few other sweet things.

Then, in a heartbreaking moment, Cole had gone up to his bedroom and brought down a photo of his family. A sweet, captured shot of a laughing family in a park, all giggles and sunshine. He pulled a second sheet of paper from the pile on the kitchen table and placed the photo on it. "This goes on the other list," he'd said quietly.

"It does," she replied. It was important to let Cole speak his grief out loud and acknowledge all he'd lost. She was prepared for him to melt into sobs. She already felt a tear slide down her cheek on his behalf. He'd lost so much.

In a flash of grace, she asked him, "Could it go on both sides?" After all, someday he'd treasure all the happy memories he could retain. He'd had such a strong, loving family. The few good memories she could hang on to of her own family were priceless to her—Cole would have a treasure trove of happy memories if he could hang on to them.

The boy considered the idea for a moment. Emma had learned even very young children could have tremendous wisdom about such things. She might be their teacher, but her students had taught her so many things over the past two years.

"Maybe sometimes," he said in answer to her suggestion. He shifted the photo so that just the smallest portion of one side edged over onto the Happy List side. Emma smiled. It was, in fact, a perfect representation of what he was feeling. She was helping him. That meant everything to her, and hopefully to Cole.

As she heard Jake's truck pull into the driveway, though, Emma wondered if she had any hope of helping that man. His expression was troubled but guarded as he walked into the house. He looked like he needed to talk, but also like he wasn't going to discuss whatever he'd learned within Cole's earshot. That was the biggest reason Jake was still a mess—it was nearly impossible for him to grieve his sister as an adult with Cole continually underfoot.

Improvising, she found a children's music video on the family room television and set it to play. "Practice your drumming for a bit and then we'll think of something fun to do next." She had to get going soon. She'd delayed her appointment with a volunteer making the nativity angel wings, but still had to get there within the hour.

Drum practice relocated out of earshot, Emma returned to the kitchen to find Jake staring intently at the list. Both lists. She knew it had to hit him even harder than it had hit her. "He's processing this really well, Jake. I'm amazed. He's going to get through this. You both are."

Without a word, Jake pulled a piece of paper from his pocket. He unfolded it and showed it to her.

She looked at the three grainy images. In each, a figure stood on the overpass that stretched above Nat and Kurt's accident scene. It was an eerie image, without much detail, the person dark against the lighter landscape around him. Or her. Really, there was no way to tell anything about the person from the vague image, except that it made her skin crawl to look at it.

Why? For the same reason Jake had to be thinking. They were staring at a photograph of the person who may very well have killed Cole's parents. "Cole should never see these," she warned in a whisper.

Jake nodded, his eyes never leaving the image. She could almost feel him slipping down into the anger that always seemed to boil just below the surface with him.

"I'm not even sure you should have them," she continued. "They don't tell you anything. They just give you someone you think you can hate."

"What if I need someone to hate?"

His question made pity and concern rise in her heart. He was being honest with her—and that was important— but she wasn't sure he would take any redirection from her right now.

"It won't help." She knew that from experience. The closure of knowing whose car had hit her mother's wasn't peace. It was a stage of healing, but it wasn't healing itself.

She looked up at Jake, daring to ask what she knew would be an infuriating question. "Could you pray for the person in this picture?"

"No!" he started to shout, then caught himself. "Are you out of your mind?"

"I didn't say forgive, or like, or help, or even not hate. You can't help but hate whoever did this. But not forever. And it won't stop by itself. You have to take it apart, piece by piece. Otherwise it swallows you."

He narrowed his eyes at her. "Did Perkins call you or something?"

"Why?"

"He said the same thing when I asked for a copy of these images."

"He's right. What's the point of having this picture? What does it give you?"

She watched Jake's fingers curl around the paper with a fierce grip. She understood his craving for justice to be done, but this image wasn't a path to that justice. "I want it to be him." His words were dark and demanding. "I want to know we'll get him and he'll pay."

Emma chose to hold his gaze, powerful as it was. "And what will you do if you don't get that?"

His expression changed, as surprised by her challenge as she was.

"*I* got that," she went on boldly. "And I'll tell you, it didn't help much." She wasn't quite sure where this surge of assertion came from. No, that was wrong. She did know its source—it was the growing urge to fight for him. To do anything she could to help Jake come out of this tragedy better than Sam had. "In fact, I'm not sure it helped at all. It certainly won't help Cole even if you think it will help you."

Jake turned away for a moment, seemingly wrestling with what she'd told him. Emma fought the urge to backpedal or apologize. She spoke the truth, hard-won from experience, and that was never anything to be ashamed of.

When he turned, most of the dark edge was gone from his eyes. The way he stared at her caused the floor to drop out from underneath her, making her acutely aware that they were alone in the kitchen together. She really ought to watch herself more carefully. Her brain—or more frighteningly, her heart—wandered too easily to places it ought not to go when she was alone with him.

His eyes had a way of clouding her thoughts and making her second-guess her plans.

"I figured something out at the police station." His tone was too warm.

"What was that?"

"I figured out how I'd be pretty much sunk if you weren't around."

Emma felt her face flush. "That's not true." The words had none of the strength she would have liked.

"It is. I'm the last person who should be helping Cole through this. I'm terrible at it. I'm just like you said—a giant ball of anger craving revenge. And you're right, it's not what Cole needs. I'm not sure I can be what Cole needs. Not without you showing me how."

Emma had no idea how to respond to a speech like that. It hit so close to her heart, spoke so strongly to her desire to help him heal, to save someone the way she couldn't seem to save Sam, that it chased away any words. Was Jake talking about grief and healing, or had he just made a declaration of sorts? She absolutely wasn't ready to take things to a different place between them. But his words woke her up to the fact that a part of her—an alarmingly large part of her—wanted to do just that.

And that was a terrible, dangerous idea, no matter how the look in his eyes called to her.

Jake seemed to sense that he'd gone too far. "I'm just saying—" he pushed the words out quickly, almost like an apology "—don't let Norma and her silly friends make you think you're doing anything wrong..."

"I'm *not* doing anything wrong," she countered, but the insistence of her own words revealed that her feelings had already wandered past a professional line.

"You're not." He shook his hand in the direction of the town as if to emphasize the point. "You're saving us."

Oh, how she wished he hadn't used those words. *You're saving us.* His declaration sank to the darkest corner of her wounded heart and refused to leave.

"You are. You're giving us the help we—I—need to do this. I gotta get this right, and I can't do that without you, no matter whether or not Norma thinks you make a good director. You're a great teacher. Because you care. And not too much, because there's no such thing. You'll be a fabulous director for the same reason. And anyone who says otherwise is going to get a piece of my mind."

Emma didn't know what he was going to say next. She only knew she needed to leave now before her defenses against his words fell down any further. She grabbed for her handbag. "You're so kind to say that." She tried to make her words sound light and polite, not born of the giant lump of emotion filling her throat just now. She was falling for him.

"I'm not kind, I'm right. Don't pull back, Emma. Not on us. Not now." She could see it in his eyes—she wasn't the only one falling. This couldn't be allowed, but how could she stop what had already started?

Pull back. It was exactly what she needed to do. Keep her focus on helping Cole as his teacher, and do whatever it took not to give in to what she was coming to feel for Jake.

"Pastor Newton can help you, too, you know." It felt like a cop-out, but she felt as if she had to say something to the pleading in his eyes.

"Goodbye, Cole!" she called loudly as she pulled her keys from her purse. "See you at school for the Christmas party Friday?"

Cole came barreling into the kitchen and hugged her legs, even with the drum still hanging from his neck. "Bye, Miss Emma. Love you."

Now the lump in her throat had no chance of staying contained. "I love you, too, sweetheart," she managed, although she wasn't sure how she got the words out. She blew him an awkward kiss, making sure she didn't meet Jake's eyes as she dashed for the door.

It took everything Emma had to walk calmly to her car. Because she wanted to run.

Chapter Thirteen

"Look at these costumes!" Celia crowed Saturday morning when she drove up for a visit. She held up the adorable glittery halos that would grace the heads of the angels. "You're going to be a big hit, you know that, don't you?"

"Maybe," Emma replied. "I'm almost back on schedule. I've got the school Christmas party behind me, so now I've just got to get through the living nativity tomorrow night. And all the other stuff."

Celia raised a dubious eyebrow. "Other stuff. So I'm not here just to ogle halos, am I?"

Emma put the costumes back on the rack. She hated that she looked over Celia's shoulder to see if the classroom door was shut, but she had to be careful. "Well, no."

Celia took a nearby chair. "What's up? Am I here to listen to the heartwarming story of Jake rescuing you from the flu? Because that would be worth the drive."

Emma was sorry she'd gone on a bit too long about how bachelor uncle Jake had gone way above and beyond the call of duty in taking care of her that morning. Celia had picked up on the attraction Emma was trying so hard to tamp down, and her friend wasn't the kind to let something like that go.

"Not that." Emma tucked the halos back into their nest of tissue paper. "It's Sam."

Celia frowned. "I think I'd much rather hear about Jake."

"I got another postcard last week," Emma persisted. "Sam signed it this time." She sat down beside Celia. "He hasn't signed the others."

"That's progress, isn't it? I mean, you've known the cards were from him all along, but he actually put his name to that one."

"I suppose. But yesterday I got another one." Emma had to tell herself to pull this latest one from her bag on the desk beside her. Her gut tightened as she handed it to Celia.

It was a drawing like all the others, a bit more disorganized and harsh, but with the same red swath across one side. She watched Celia scan the card until her eyes hit on the trio of words tucked into the corner of the drawing. The spot where small, unsteady letters spelled out *I've done something.*

"What do you think *I've done something* means?" Celia asked.

Emma pushed out a breath. "I have no idea."

Celia flipped the card over, looking for additional clues the same way Emma had done yesterday when it arrived in her mailbox. "Could be anything. Could be he's gone someplace new to get help. Or climbed a mountain. Or ordered a pizza—who knows?" She handed the card back to Emma. "It could be an announcement to make you proud of him."

Emma forced out the words she'd been holding back. "Or maybe it's a confession."

Celia's brows furrowed. "Stop that. Don't go there. You'll make yourself nuts thinking like that."

"Well, I'm worried."

"Of course you're worried. Sam's a mess. He probably thinks you don't know he checked himself out of Bowman Hills. Emma, we've been over this a dozen times. He's a grown man and you have no leverage over him, legally or otherwise." She fixed Emma with a hard stare. "You're not responsible for him. You never were."

"I don't know what *I've done something* means. I don't know anything." Emma's frustration seemed to grab at her chest with tight fingers. "Why won't he let me know where he is?"

"Because he doesn't want to. He doesn't want your help, Emma. At least, not right now."

Emma told herself Celia was right. She'd restricted communication with Sam because his drama and instability were hijacking her life. He never seemed to want to heal—he only seemed intent on pulling her down with him into the pit he'd dug for himself. Cutting herself off had been the right choice then, and it was still the right choice now. Wasn't it? But it was Christmas. Sam shouldn't be alone at Christmas.

"You've been happier these past two years in Wander Canyon than I've ever seen you," Celia went on. "Part of that is because Sam isn't sucking you into his mess. You know that's the truth. And that's *not bad*. Or selfish."

Emma looked away from her friend's insistent eyes. She had fought long and hard to overcome the guilt of stepping away from Sam. How had he erased all that progress with a handful of postcards? If Sam really had done something horrible, wouldn't it be at least partly her fault? The result of the attention she'd denied him? "But the postmarks. He's leaving me clues."

"No, he's not. He's not that clever." Celia shifted to face Emma directly. "Don't let him do this to you, Emma. Look, Sam knows where you are. He can reach you if he needs you. But he's chosen not to let you know where he is. *He's* chosen that."

"But…"

"But nothing. Even if you think he needs you, he clearly doesn't want it." Celia put a hand over Emma's. "You've done everything you can. It's gonna have to be enough. Live your life instead of trying to fix Sam's. His isn't fixable. At least not now, and not by you."

Celia was right. Her friend could always see things with Sam so much more clearly than Emma could. Her emotions always tangled things up—much like with Jake. Who was she to lecture Jake on his anger when her own guilt was causing just as much trouble for her?

Emma hugged her friend. "Where would I be without you?" The words struck her as an echo of the sentiment Jake had expressed earlier. The attraction between them was in danger of going beyond one person helping another through a difficult time. Actually, when she was honest with herself, it already had gone beyond that. Why was everything coming at her all at once? Now?

"You'd be fine," Celia encouraged. "You'd be amazing because you already are. Don't you ever think of yourself as some kind of failure because Sam can't pull himself together."

Wasn't that exactly what she'd been doing? Letting Sam's mess of a life define hers? Giving it even more power by thinking it had to be a carefully guarded secret?

After all, she'd told Jake, and he hadn't thought less of her because of it. He wasn't making any secret of his growing feelings for her—and she didn't think she was doing a very good job of hiding her growing feelings for him.

Celia gestured to the costumes hanging around them. "Look at this. Look at the happy memories you're going to give these kids and their families. This whole thing is straight out of a cheesy, wonderful Christmas movie. And that's thanks to you."

Despite a rocky start, the living nativity plans did look like they were going to come together. She was quick to catalog everything that had gone wrong, but so much had gone well. "I guess it will be nice when it all works out."

"Nice?" Celia teased. "It'll be incredible. Because you're incredible. God's done a massive thing in your life, Emma. Think about that. To come out of the messed-up childhood you and Sam had, and grow up to be someone who makes children happy?" She grabbed one of the sparkly halos and held it over Emma's head. "This belongs on you."

The grip on Emma's chest loosened. "Actually, it belongs on Maddie Walker." She gave Celia a hug. "Thanks. I was really getting spooked by this whole card thing."

"I would say he's just pushing your buttons, but I don't even think it's that deliberate. He's messed up, but I don't think he's malicious. Just let it go and focus on where you *can* do good—right here."

She could give the children wonderful Christmas memories. She could help the whole town, actually, because while the living nativity was really for the kids, the cast was mostly adults. More importantly, she could give Cole something close to a nice Christmas. She was one of the few people who knew how, because of her messed-up childhood. God was hopefully showing her how to take that mess and use it for good, not let it damage her the way it had Sam.

"I've always thought that maybe it's exactly why God led me here. For Cole."

Celia smiled. "No maybe about it, if you ask me. But would it be so awful if it was also for Jake?"

Jake sipped a cup of coffee and looked out the window Sunday evening. It was a picture-perfect December night for Emma's living nativity. "You're missing a good one," he whispered to Natalie's memory. She'd always been a fan of the sort of soft, fluffy snow that fell tonight under a bright moon.

He looked over at the small tree he and Emma had managed to set up by the living room window. Without her help, the thing might have looked pathetic. As it was, it somehow fit in Natalie's beautifully decorated home. The house felt like Christmas, and that alone was a monumental feat, even if every decoration lodged a lump in Jake's throat. Four days left, and it looked like they were going to actually make it through. If that wasn't a Christmas blessing, he didn't know what was.

Cole padded into the living room. "Do I hafta wear long johns?"

The biblical-looking tunic and pants weren't enough to keep Cole warm on a night like this. "You'll freeze if you don't."

Cole picked up the *Little Drummer Boy* picture book Grandma Sarah had sent. She was so sad to miss Cole's appearance, but Jake had promised to capture it on his cell phone and send it. Sarah had suggested they go to her house for Christmas since she couldn't yet travel, but

Jake wasn't sure they would make the trip. Too much had changed to add Christmas somewhere else to the mix. Jake found himself craving the familiarity of his church home this Christmas and suspected Cole felt the same on some level. Besides, it was starting to feel like they were actually getting the hang of things.

Cole pointed to the little boy on the cover of his book. "*He's* not wearing long johns."

"He's in the middle of the desert. Christmas is warm where Jesus comes from." Jake would add this to the hundred other absurd conversations he'd had as a stand-in parent. Right up there with "No, you can't feed turtles peanut butter," and "It's not okay to wear pajamas to school even if it's blue day and your jammies are blue."

Cole's lower lip stuck out. "I feel stupid."

"In an hour you'll feel warm and be glad you knew to wear long johns." It struck Jake at that moment that he was starting to sound like a parent. *Yikes.*

Cole's lip began to tremble. This was about more than thermal underwear. Jake set down the coffee mug he was holding. "Whoa, buddy, what's wrong?"

A long, aching pause hung in the air until Cole said, "Mom's not here."

The ever-present cracking sensation in Jake's chest split wide open. Grief had become a physical sensation, a tangible, splitting jab that could steal his breath and stop him in his tracks. He pulled his nephew into his arms. "No, she's not. And that hurts, doesn't it?"

"I miss her and Dad." Cole cried into Jake's chest, small ribs heaving inside the tight circle of Jake's arms.

"I know you do," Jake said, feeling his own breath come hard. "I know you do. I do, too." Natalie's loss was so huge. It touched everything about his life right now.

The emotional grief of losing the only thing that felt like family to him was compounded by all the practical fall-out from Nat and Kurt being gone. He was beyond weary of coping, holding it together, trying to be a functioning human being when he felt like a pointless puddle most days. Most hours.

In all honesty, he felt like sitting in the middle of the living room floor and throwing a good tantrum right alongside Cole. To yell loudly and hit something. Every cell in his body still felt sore and angry.

None of that would help Cole. And he had to help Cole. It was up to him to guide the little guy through this. How? That word continually dogged him like a hungry wolf. *How?*

He let Cole cry a little bit, guessing it was better to get it out now. Jake wondered if maybe this drummer boy gig was just beyond Cole right now, and considered phoning Emma to say Cole wasn't going to make it to-night. But he also had to show Cole that life could, and would, and ought to go on.

As he felt the wet spot on his shoulder grow larger, Jake looked past Cole toward the kitchen. Emma had put Cole's Happy and Sad List up, instructing Jake to let Cole add a drawing of anything he wanted to—even if it made no sense. *Every time you can,* he heard her voice in his head, *show him how there are more happy things than sad ones. Or at least that there are things on both sides.*

Emma's advice gave Jake an idea. When Cole seemed to have cried it out, Jake turned them both toward the window. "It's okay to be sad. But look outside at the snow. Looks pretty nice, doesn't it?"

"It's the fluffy kind."

That was exactly how Nat had always described it.

"Sure is," he said, scooting them closer to the window. "That was always your mom's favorite kind of snow, wasn't it? The really pretty fluffy kind like the stuff outside tonight."

Cole nodded.

"You know what I think? I think maybe she sent it. Mom wanted you to have her favorite kind of snow for tonight." Even his own sore heart liked the idea of Natalie sending a picture-perfect snowfall to grace the evening. He didn't know if it was sound reasoning—and he didn't much care. He and Cole were making this up as they went along, and anything that got them through a tough moment was a good thing.

It happened then, just like Emma said it would. Jake felt the boil of anger simmer down. He let her idea—the one that there could be good things in the midst of all this struggle—settle into his chest and push out the darkness. He'd never really bought into her idea that gratitude could push back against the grief until just this moment. It was something he did for Cole, not for himself. Emma really was amazing. A Godsend, in the truest sense of the word. She'd be at the top of his Happy List, if he had one. Maybe he'd draft one and show it to her.

"Will Mom and Dad hear me?" Cole touched the drum with his chubby hand.

"I think so," Jake said with all the certainty he could muster. "And you know what? They'll be bursting with pride. Just like me." He pulled the boy into a hug and realized the most important thing he could say on a night like tonight. "I love you, Cole. Heaps and heaps and forever." He should say it more often. He probably couldn't say it enough in the next four days. In the next four years.

"I love you, too, Uncle Jake." The words were sweet

and warm against Jake's chest. This moment would go on his Happy List, too. *That's two*, he thought, his heart warming further for the tenderhearted teacher who was teaching him as much as she taught his nephew.

He kissed the top of Cole's head, not caring that it was the gooiest of displays. "Wanna draw some snow on your Happy List before we head out?"

"Yep," Cole replied, brightening. "Purple snow."

Why not purple snow? Nothing about tonight would look like any other Christmas, after all. Standing up, Jake walked over to the kitchen drawer and fished out a purple crayon. He handed it to Cole with great ceremony. "Purple it is." He watched with genuine pride and a surge of affection as Cole carefully drew fat, purple, starlike snowflakes on the Happy side of the list. Then, in a gesture that threatened to break Jake's heart wide open all over again, Cole planted a fat kiss on the photo of his mother and father that sat in the middle of the two lists. With a smile.

Maybe, just maybe, they would make it through this holiday. He had Emma to thank for that. He had Emma to thank for a lot of things. He'd find a way to tell her that tonight.

Maybe he'd also find a way to tell her how he felt. It was nearly Christmas, after all.

Chapter Fourteen

Emma stood with a clipboard in the back portico of Wander Canyon Community Church. The wide outside overhang had been pressed into service as "backstage" for the crèche.

"Shepherds over here. Each of you gets a crook. Mark, I'm counting on you to keep a hold of that leash on that lamb."

As if to protest Emma's lack of confidence, the sheep gave a loud bleat and an enthusiastic leap.

"On it," Mark Volker, the true shepherd of the cast since he actually owned the sheep, replied. "Cotton won't get out of hand." Cotton, on the other hand, chose to show her feelings on cooperation by biting down on the strap of the little bag strung around Mark's waist and tugging hard enough to nearly knock the man over. Evidently gaining Cotton's obedience was going to require a steady supply of the sheep treats—whatever those were—inside that bag.

One of the angels laughed. "He's hungry."

Zosia came around from the front of the church. "I've plugged in the manger heating pad as well as the overhead heating lamps. Baby Jesus, Joseph and Mary should be nice and toasty and out of the wind. They're inside by the front door, and we'll bring them out last. Little Logan's been fed and changed so he ought to sleep in heavenly peace all night." She pulled her mittens from her coat pocket. "The rest of us will just have to make do. It's not a bad night at all, by winter standards anyhow." She looked out at the beautiful swirl of falling snowflakes. "And beyond pretty."

Emma thanked her stage manager with a hug. "Cole told me his mama sent the pretty snow. I had to fight back a tear after that one."

"How's little Cole doing?"

"Jake told me they had a rough moment just before leaving, but Cole seems to be okay. Keep an eye on him for me, will you? If it gets to be too much, I want him to feel okay to go home."

A loud moo pulled Emma's attention to where Hank Walker was leading a pair of cows out of a trailer. "Where do you want your lowing cattle?" he asked with a grin.

Emma handed him his robe, belt and head scarf. "Out front, by the fence on the left-hand side."

Hank nodded as he began leading the beasts toward the front of the church. "Come on, gals. Time for your theatrical debut."

Pauline Walker came up to Emma with open hands. "I'm here to help. What needs doing?"

Emma checked her clipboard. "Angel halos. There are some hair clips in the box with them. Tell the girls they can leave their hats on if they're cold."

"Thanks, by the way," Pauline said with a wink. "Hank and I are tickled pink that Wyatt's playing Joseph. Chaz was a fine choice, but Wyatt as a stand-in is nothing short of brilliant."

Emma wasn't sure Wyatt agreed with that, but she offered Pauline a smile anyway. "How's that grandnephew of yours?"

Pauline beamed. "Just the most perfect baby boy in the whole world. Toni ought to thank me. I'm pretty sure I bought out every single baby boy holiday item in her store this year."

"Miss Emma!" A shout from over by the Wise Men demanded Emma's attention. "We got a problem over here!"

"You go get everyone ready," Pauline said. "I'll tackle the angels and their angel hair. Ha! Angel hair. Pasta, get it?" The old woman chuckled at her own joke as she walked off in the direction of the heavenly hosts.

Three torn costumes, one hastily replaced feverish Wise Man and a broken shepherd's crook later, Emma followed her cast of humans around the outside of the church to move into their places amidst the animals in the stable Jake had built. As they took their positions, the lights illuminated the snow falling lightly around them. Oohs and ahhs floated up from the crowd that had gathered for the occasion, and the choir began to sing "Silent Night."

"Look at that," Pastor Newton said in genuine admiration as he walked up to stand next to Emma. "What a perfect blessing it all is." He smiled at her, and Emma felt a glow that had nothing to do with the lights. Here in front of her was a lovely Christmas memory for everyone to hold dear. All the striving, arguing, sewing and scrambling felt worth it. She'd made a difference. It really felt like a perfect blessing.

Until the spunky lamb decided to slip from her harness and jump the fence, causing Mark to yell, "Sorry!" to Emma as he sprinted off across the church lawn in pursuit of his fleecy escapee. Emma told herself to pay no heed to the sour face Norma Binton made at the mishap. The night was bound to have one or two, and this one was minor. She simply forced a smile in Norma's direction as the little lamb was returned—bleating a loud protest—to the scene.

Everything was settled back in place just in time for Joseph, Mary and a carefully swaddled Baby Jesus to emerge and take their places as the choir began "Away in a Manger." Emma couldn't say for sure if Hank Walker had somehow prodded his cows to begin lowing at the exact moment the song lyrics described it, but she sent a small prayer that "the baby awakes, but little Lord Jesus no crying he makes," would hold equally true.

It did, even when the crowd broke into applause as the trio of little angels climbed the staircase to the balcony on one side of the manger and recited a poem about the Christmas Star. No one cared that little Maddie Walker's halo slipped off and fell to hang comically on the ear of one of her step-grandfather's cows below. For a shining moment, everything was perfect. Emma held her breath in the small pause that came before the choir would begin "The Little Drummer Boy" to cue Cole's appearance. She found herself yearning to see Jake's expression as the results of their work made a joyful memory for the boy they both cared about. She'd never act on it, but neither could Emma deny how much she'd come to care about both the boy and his extraordinary uncle.

Emma's thoughts were interrupted by a little girl pushing to the front of the crowd. She leaned toward Mary and said in a loud know-it-all tone, "You know that's not the real Baby Jesus, don't you?"

"Gracious!" snapped Norma. "Hush that child!"

"Cindy!" the girl's mother gasped in mortification, clamping her hand over the sassy child's mouth.

Pastor Newton, as he often did, had the perfect retort to the crowd's awkward laughter. "But it's fun to pretend, don't you think, Cindy?"

Cindy's mother looked as if she was not having any fun at all at the moment, glaring down at her daughter. Norma looked annoyed that the reverend hadn't sided with her. Emma caught the choir director's eye in a "save us" look that had him launching the choir into the lyrics, *"Come, they told me pa-rum-pa-pum-pum..."*

From the other side of the church, Cole appeared, hitting his little drum with great ceremony. Surely no finer rum-pa-pum-pum had ever been drummed. His appearance was met with enthusiastic cheering, garnering a few competitive looks from the angels who clearly felt they deserved the most applause. Jake walked several paces behind Cole, staying out of the spotlight so the boy had the moment to himself. But even the evening's growing darkness couldn't conceal the wide smile on Jake's face, nor the intensity of his gaze when it met Emma's. She couldn't stop her heart from skipping a beat—in fact, it beat with more insistence than Cole's tiny drum. When the crowd began to sing along, Emma felt as if God himself smiled down upon this tiny town and its loving support of one boy after a tragedy.

She found herself using one mitten to wipe away tears, and caught glimpses of other people doing the same. *He's okay*, she said in a prayer she hoped Kurt and Natalie could somehow hear. *He's going to be okay.* Her heart was only half surprised when she realized she was talking about both Jake and Cole.

As rehearsed, Cole finished his performance by kneeling in front of the manger. He looked appropriately adoring, until he began to wrinkle his nose. Then she noticed that Wyatt as Joseph was doing his best not to, as well. Even Carrie Binton as Mary, and now two of the shepherds, were making faces. The nearest angel decided it was time to inform her mother that "Baby Jesus smells really bad."

"What is it with these disrespectful children?" Norma sneered.

"Baby Jesus was a baby, after all," Pauline Walker pointed out. "And babies don't always smell divine."

The crowd laughed as two of the three angels decided to make a show of holding their celestial noses.

"Mary," Wyatt said to Carrie in a dramatic tone, "why don't we go to the inn for a moment and see to our holy child's…needs before any more…visitors come."

Agreeing with Wyatt's tactic, Emma held her hand up in a *halt* signal to the trio of Wise Men just coming around the corner. Unless they were toting gold, frankincense and a fresh diaper, they'd need to hold off a few minutes. She twirled one index finger at the choir director in the universal "vamp for time" signal.

Thankfully quick on the uptake, the choir began "It Came Upon a Midnight Clear."

"It seems we need a brief intermission," Pastor Newton said with a laugh.

"It seems we need a better nativity organizer," Norma shot back.

"That's it," came Jake's powerful voice from the side

of the crowd. "Norma, if you don't let up on Emma right this minute, you're gonna find out what a first-class Scrooge I can be."

Old Biddy Binton swiveled her head around so fast Jake was surprised it didn't spin right off her shoulders. He met her glare with the darkest one of his own he could muster.

She opened her mouth to launch into one of her legendary tirades, but he wasn't going to let her get one word out. Not tonight. Not after the amazing thing Emma had created here.

The crowd split apart in front of him as he walked up to the spiteful old woman. "I've had just enough of you finding fault with everything Emma does. With what everyone does. Why haven't you ever tried to lift a finger to help her out instead?"

"I have," Norma said defensively.

"No, you haven't. All you've done is nitpick every little thing you don't like. And you don't like anything." If no one else was going to call Norma on this, then he was willing to step out and do it. "All just because you want your niece to have her job."

Carrie, who hadn't yet made it offstage with the pungent Baby Jesus, had the decency to look sheepish. "No offense, Carrie," Jake offered to the young woman. "I know enough to pick my beefs with the *people who deserve it.*" He made sure those last four words were directed straight at Norma.

Norma practically snorted. "The nerve of some people!"

"My thoughts exactly," Jake shot back louder than was necessary. He was long past putting up with that old bird's mean spirit, especially tonight.

Emma pushed through the crowd, hands raised. "Jake…"

"No," he countered. "I'm sick of it, Emma. I'm sick of the way she's looked down that pointy nose of hers at all the great things you've done. I'm fed up with her gossipy ways. You're the best thing that's ever happened to…Cole and this school, and no one's gonna convince me otherwise." He barely stopped himself short of saying "to me," because it really did feel like she was the only thing holding him upright most days. Every day.

Pastor Newton stepped squarely in between Jake and Norma. "Why doesn't everyone take a breath here," he said. The reverend gave both Jake and Norma stern looks in equal measure. "I'm sure we'd all agree this is no place for an argument."

Bo and Toni suddenly appeared at Jake's side, Bo's hand grasping Jake's shoulder. "Simmer down, okay?"

"For Cole," Toni added, inclining her head slightly toward the concern on the boy's face.

Pauline Walker pulled Norma's hand into the crook of her elbow. "Come on, Norma, let's go see if the hot chocolate is ready." Despite the fact that Jake knew Wyatt had locked horns with Norma, as well, Pauline shot Jake a look that let him know he'd crossed a line.

He supposed he had. Several, in fact. Just another fault to add to the long list piling up this month. Still, he couldn't bring himself to regret the true words he'd said—just how he'd allowed his temper to get the best of him in front of Cole.

"For what it's worth," Bo said quietly, "I couldn't agree more, but this isn't the time or the place…or the audience."

Jake searched across the sea of murmuring people

until he met Emma's gaze. She looked half mortified at his outburst, and half touched by his defense of her. Or at least that's what he hoped he saw in her expression. *I meant it*, he tried to say across the distance. He had a dozen things he wanted to say to her right now, but as Bo pointed out, this wasn't the time or the place. *Don't let it end here*, Jake prayed as he forced a slow exhale from his chest and watched the mist of his breath hang in the frosty air. *Give me a chance to talk to her.*

Jake was starting to walk toward Emma when he felt Bo's hand clamp down harder on his shoulder. "Let Emma handle this." Bo's advice came quietly over his shoulder.

Five very uncomfortable minutes later the Holy Family returned from its diaper change session to settle back into place as if nothing had happened. Jake watched Emma set her shoulders to carry on. "Your visitors are about to arrive," she declared to Wyatt in a confident *let's get on with it* tone Jake had to admire. *Good for you*, he thought. *Don't you let this nativity get sidelined by Norma or me or anything.*

Cole gave the returning baby a little drum greeting. Emma pointed to the choir director, who started the singers into a round of "We Three Kings of Orient Are." A loud braying filled the night air as Ed, the town barber, now dressed as one of the "wise guys," appeared, yanking a reluctant donkey around the corner toward the manger.

And so the rest of the Christmas story unfolded without incident. Well, without *major* incident. The sheep never quite left off trying to eat the shepherd's costume, Baby Jesus indulged in a small crying fit when presented with his gold and the Christmas Star got caught in a stiff breeze and nearly swung off its mounting into the crowd. All in all, Jake found himself with a host of funny and heartwarming new memories to battle all the sadness that loomed over the coming Christmas. As the crowd applauded and the cast headed back behind the church to remove their costumes, Jake made a promise to himself. *I'm going to make sure Emma knows how much tonight meant to me. How much she means to me.*

Could he cross that bridge tonight? Defy her insistence that what he felt couldn't be acted upon? Because there was no mistaking the feelings. Not his, or hers—because he knew she felt something, too. None of her denying words outweighed the constant pull gaining strength between them—off-limits or otherwise.

Jake was never good at off-limits anyway. Or doing what he was told. And he didn't want to start tonight.

Leaving Cole in the company of some classmates and their parents polishing off Christmas cookies and hot chocolate, Jake searched the church until he found her in the classroom with all the costumes. She was alone, out of sight of anyone who might make her think twice about talking to him. Jake took that as a green light and stepped into the room. "That was nothing short of amazing, Emma."

She spun around at the greeting, her eyes wide. It shocked him to see she'd been crying. Crying? Sure, things had gone wrong, but from where he stood, she'd just had a huge victory over a mountain of obstacles. Pulling the door shut quietly behind him, Jake rushed to her side, not caring how close it put him. In fact, he enjoyed that she didn't object when he put a hand on her arm. "Seriously, it was. What's wrong?"

She waved away her tears. "Silly, I know."

He'd fought plenty of emotions he would have classified as silly in the past weeks. "You pulled it off. The whole thing was incredible. Why are you crying?"

She looked up at him in that moment, and Jake felt the oddest sensation in his chest, as if his heart had up and left without his permission. Appropriate or not, he'd fallen for her. Hard.

"I was so sure it wouldn't make a difference," she said, her voice wavering in a way that made him itch to pull her into his arms. He knew from that moment in the woods that she fit perfectly against his chest. He began to crave the moment she'd feel ready to return his embrace.

She sniffed and went on. "I was hoping I could just make a nice little Christmas thing without too much going wrong."

How could she think what she'd done was only "a nice little Christmas thing"?

"It's more," he insisted, finding the two words woefully insufficient. He found the contact of his hand on her arm woefully insufficient, as well, but forced himself to keep still. She had all this strength but was delicate in ways that made it hard to stop wanting to protect her. Hard to stop thinking about her, period. "Are you kidding? It's a huge thing. Huge."

"A ton of things went wrong."

"Who cares? I don't. And I don't think anyone else does because *so much* of it went right."

"I know that. Really, I do."

Jake could live to be a hundred and never figure women out. "So…?"

"It's just that…" She sniffed again, eyes still wide in a disbelief he couldn't understand. "I'm…happy. I didn't think I could be happy. Not at Christmas."

She'd told him her mother died in December. Had it darkened her Christmas every year after that? He knew Natalie's death would for him—and regretfully for Cole—but he'd always figured she'd found a way out of that darkness. Otherwise, how could she have guided him as wisely as she had?

Or maybe, just maybe, he could have been a tiny part of that happiness? "I get that. You know I do." Every part of Jake wanted to wipe away her tears, but instead he offered what he hoped was his warmest smile and handed her Cole's little head scarf. He'd tucked it into his pocket when Cole yanked it off his head because it got in the way of eating cookies. It wasn't much of a gentleman's handkerchief, but he figured she wouldn't mind.

"Tonight was a happy memory," he went on. "For Cole and for me. I didn't think that was possible." Emma's eyes glowed for a minute, and the combination of them glowing and glistening with tears went straight through Jake's chest like a lightning bolt. He knew for sure now—she did feel it. That thing humming between them pulled both ways.

Unwise or not, unsafe or not, he dared to add, "Before you came along."

Chapter Fifteen

Of all the things Jake could say to capture her heart, why did he have to say that? Now? With an astonishment that nearly made her knees buckle, Emma thought that if he leaned in and kissed her, she'd let him. She'd sink into his arms and even kiss him back. And it would be wonderful.

…And it might cost her this job.

But more than that, it would pull the rug out from underneath the peace and stability she desperately needed right now. As caring as Jake was—and he was capable of great caring, she knew that now—he was a wild card. An impulsive, reckless man who was up to his knees in his own problems. Even without the professional complications, she needed strong and steady. And while Jake was fascinating and distractingly handsome and sweet in ways that continually surprised her, he wasn't strong and steady.

He was also persistent. She needed him to let up on the intensity of his gaze. "I didn't realize it was still so hard for you. Which is dumb of me. I mean, I feel like it will be hard forever. I just thought you'd figured out how to stop it from hurting somehow."

Emma told him the truth. "It will always hurt. I've only figured out a way to live with it so it doesn't show so much."

"Even out the Happy and Sad sides?" His eyes told her he understood what she'd been teaching Cole. And as he told her the story of the snow and Cole's drawing of the snowflakes, the last of Emma's resistance to this man began to melt like springtime snow. When he stepped closer to her, most of her shouted to step back and put some distance between them. That part didn't win as she remembered the lure of his arms around her in the woods, strong and comforting. Defiant in a way she hadn't realized she needed.

As if he'd read her mind, Jake took a step closer and said, "I don't care what Norma thinks. Or anyone else."

"I have to," she retorted, sounding as unconvinced as she felt.

"Are you sure?"

She wasn't sure at all. Or she was ready to ignore all the reasons she should care. It was Christmas. She was just the tiniest bit happy for the first time in forever. Shouldn't that count for something? Didn't the Happy side of her list get to matter, just for now?

She felt Jake's hand slide up her arm, and her heart actually did that flipping thing everyone always talked about. They were in an ordinary classroom, surrounded by piles of tossed costumes, but the air felt as wondrous as if angel halos filled the skies. Maybe she had let Norma's rules have too much say in her life. She deserved to have personal happiness alongside any professional achievements, didn't she?

Jake's hand came up to her cheek, and with one thumb he tenderly wiped the wet path of her tears. This time she really did think her knees would give way, and the enthralling thought that she'd tumble into his arms made it impossible to breathe. The thrill of leaning just the slightest bit toward him felt dizzying.

Until the door clicked open behind Jake. "Hey, Emma…" came Zosia's voice until she skidded to a stop, mouth open and eyes wide, in the classroom doorway.

For a moment, no one seemed to know what to say. Jake stepped back quickly, stuffing his hands in his pockets like a guilty schoolchild. Emma dearly hoped her cheeks didn't look like they were burning, because they certainly felt as if they were.

"I didn't realize I was interrupting." Emma searched for either understanding or condemnation in Zosia's tone, but couldn't read either.

"You weren't," Jake said at the same time Emma said, "Not at all." The double denial only dug them in further.

"I can come back," Zosia said, backing out the way she came.

"No," Emma insisted. Disappointment warred with gratitude in her chest. It might have been a splendid kiss, but that wouldn't have changed the risk it would have been.

"Just returning Cole's head scarf thing," Jake explained, nodding toward the cloth in Emma's hand.

"Couldn't it wait for the rest of his costume? I just left him wearing it at the cookie table." Was Zosia teasing?

Jake made a wide arc around Zosia as he bolted for the door. "Speaking of the little guy, I'd better go fetch him before he devours a pound of sugar. Thanks again, Emma," he added, somehow making his voice sound parental, in distinct contrast to the very personal thanks he'd just given her. "Great job."

As Jake rushed out the door, and Zosia stared after him, Emma sat down on the edge of one of the classroom tables, the air stunned out of her.

Zosia turned slowly and walked farther into the classroom. "Are we going to talk about that?"

"No." Emma gulped.

"Oh, we *are* going to talk about that," Zosia declared, her voice the mixture of tender and firm that made her such an excellent teacher. She sat down next to Emma. "Risky waters there."

"No kidding."

"Some people have very strict rules about teacher–parent relationships. Children have to be protected. There can't be too much caution about these things."

Emma nodded. Her whole body shook a little bit, as if she'd just been yanked back from the edge of a very high cliff. Hadn't she?

"And then there's Cole to think about. He's in a very vulnerable place right now. You could do more harm than good."

"I know that."

Zosia sighed. "I think you should be the director. You know that."

Zosia had always stood strong in that opinion. Emma valued her support tremendously. Even the best kiss in the world wasn't worth risking that. "I appreciate you so much, Zosia. I'd never do anything to…"

Zosia cut her off. "Relax. What I just saw—or what I'm pretty sure I was just about to see—doesn't change that." Zosia hiked her small body up to sit fully on the table. "I do think we need to be careful about such things, but I also see this as an unusual situation. It could be special. It could also be disastrous. The timing couldn't be worse."

Relief flooded Emma's chest. She hadn't lost Zosia's confidence in that moment of almost giving in to the powerful allure of Jake's eyes. "I feel like so much is at stake. I... I'm not sure I trust myself to make a good decision."

"Would it help you to know that I do? One of your best gifts to this school is your instinct. You've come up with ways to help Cole that aren't in any textbook." She shifted a bit to look more directly at Emma. "What's your intuition telling you now?"

Emma pushed out a breath. "A hundred things. And none of them agree. Jake is..." she reached for the words to describe the tumult she was feeling "...growing on me." It seemed an oversimplification, but her head wasn't clear enough to do the subject justice. "He feels like he could be important." *He feels like he could be wonderful.* Emma shook her head. "There's definitely something there. But just because it's there doesn't mean I should act on it."

"No, it doesn't," Zosia replied. "But it doesn't mean you have to ignore it, either."

"Oh, believe me, I don't think I can ignore it." Emma surprised herself with the confession. "He surprised me. I didn't expect him to be so good with Cole. Or to try so hard." She leaned back on her hands as they sat side by side on the table. Somehow the conversation had stopped being between a teacher and her boss and now felt like one between two friends. One wise friend and one confused friend. "He's caught me off guard, I suppose."

"If I hadn't walked in, would he have kissed you?"

That was Zosia—she never shied away from addressing a topic head-on.

There wasn't much point in denying it. "I think so." When Zosia raised an eyebrow, Emma amended it to, "Yes."

"It certainly looked that way to me." Zosia gave her an understanding smile before crossing one leg over the other. "But that's not the problem. The problem—if you want to call it that—is that it would have looked that way to Norma or anyone else. Now might not be the time to give anyone reason to question your integrity or judgment."

"I totally agree." There might be a time and place to take things up with Jake; it just wasn't now. Most of her knew that. It was just the other smitten, lonely part of her that refused to play by the rules.

"I'd say I totally agree, too…if it weren't for the fact that I've never seen you look happier than you just did a moment ago. Your happiness has to count for something, too. The Normas of the world can be right and be all wrong, you know. There's a difference between judgment and wisdom."

Emma hadn't met too many people wiser than Zosia. It shocked her just a bit to see Zosia seemingly in favor of her pursuing things with Jake. "So you're okay with… this?" She wasn't even sure what "this" was, let alone knowing Zosia's opinion of it.

"I'm in favor of your happiness. I don't know if that includes Jake Sanders or not. That's pretty much going to be up to you. Do you think you can be thoughtful and careful about this?"

Jake had just taken her breath away, and he hadn't even tried to kiss her. Yet. "I'm not sure."

"It's hard to be careful about things like this." Zosia grinned. "I was young once, too, you know."

Emma was struck by a wave of insecurity. As the director, could she be this wise? People would look to her the way she looked to Zosia. Was she truly ready for that? Or had tonight been God's way of showing her she wasn't?

"What should I do?" The question seemed so weak, so un-director-like.

"My advice is not to act on what you're feeling until you can do it thoughtfully."

Tonight, that felt a dozen years away. Emma's heart was still racing from the glow in Jake's eyes and the gentle touch he'd given her cheek.

"Which might mean," Zosia went on, "that it would be wise not to get in situations where it's just you and Jake and your...uncareful...feelings."

"I'm still helping to take care of Cole. How am I going to do that?"

Zosia pushed herself off the table and gave Emma a warm hug. "I said it was wise. I didn't say it would be easy."

Monday morning Jake set down his saw in disgust. He'd cut this angle three times and still hadn't gotten it right. The small job of setting molding around the new door frame for the Chamber of Commerce should have been a twenty-minute process, and he'd been here over an hour. Nat's library wasn't looking like it was going to be ready by December thirtieth, and he didn't have this kind of time to squander on stupid mistakes.

Bo looked up from his own task. "Everything okay?"

Jake could only shrug. Everything was not okay. The

fog around him that he kept hoping would clear only seemed to thicken when he wasn't looking. He felt too much about too many things to be clearheaded about even the simplest of tasks. "Grief brain," Pastor Newton had called it, but Jake knew it was more than that. It was grief brain and Cole brain and Emma brain and a dozen other brains. *Half brain*, he joked to himself, frowning at the lumber he'd wasted in the last thirty minutes.

More like full-on Emma brain. He couldn't stop thinking about her, and in ways that had nothing to do with tending to Cole. He'd been infatuated with women before, but Emma represented some kind of vital lifeline to him. When had he started to think that he'd never be able to make life work without her? He considered himself a free spirit—the notion of dependence that deep made his skin itch. Could he trust what he was feeling? Or was this just some odd fallout from how much he missed Natalie?

Jake looked up to see Bo staring at him. How long had he been lost in thought? That seemed to happen all the time lately—he'd drift off to places in the middle of tasks and conversations. The other night he pulled into the driveway with no clear memory of the drive home from work. And he'd lost track of the number of times Cole had poked him for spacing out in the middle of reading their nightly books.

Leaning against the wall, Jake offered an apologetic smile to his partner. "I feel like my brain cells are leaking out. I miss stuff. I space out. I forget things. That's not me. You know that—or I hope you do."

"Actually," Bo said, "I'm pretty amazed you're doing as well as you are. What you're handling? It's huge. A lesser guy would be falling to pieces."

Who says I'm not falling to pieces? Just the fact that his brain came up with thoughts like that proved Jake's own point. "I don't feel anything close to amazing," he admitted. But he'd used that exact word to describe Emma last night, hadn't he? Amazing. She was. She amazed him. He would have ignored every prudent boundary and kissed her last night in that classroom. He still couldn't decide if he was ticked or thankful Zosia had interrupted.

Bo walked over and picked up the saw Jake had tossed aside. "How about you duck over to the Depot and get us both a cup of coffee while I finish this up?"

Jake couldn't argue. Irritating as it was, the fastest way to the completion of this job was to hand it off to Bo. At least his partner had given him a way to save face—and a good strong cup of coffee would go down great after the trouble he'd had sleeping last night.

"I like that plan."

As he walked toward the Depot, a little coffee shop housed in an old train car that sat close to Wander Canyon's iconic carousel, Jake halted. He fished in his back pants pocket to discover the permission slip he'd been supposed to turn in to school this morning. Emma had offered to take it in for him, but he'd insisted that as a grown man he was capable of turning in a single sheet of paper on time.

Evidently not. He was failing spectacularly at this parenting thing, and Cole was paying the price. Even with Emma's help he wasn't able to hold it together. He was the sorriest of stand-ins for Nat and Kurt. He wasn't even a decent substitute for Grandma Sarah.

As he stood waiting for the coffees, feeling his spirit sink, he felt a touch to his shoulder and turned to see Marilyn Walker. "Hi, Jake. How are you holding up?"

Jake still couldn't tell if people wanted the true answer

to that question. Knowing Marilyn had been widowed at an early age, he opted for honesty. "Miserably, actually." He motioned toward an open table as the young woman behind the counter handed off the set of coffees. "Got a minute?" Bo probably wouldn't mind if Jake kept his incompetent self off the job site for a bit longer.

Marilyn's smile was warm and understanding as she nodded. "As a matter of fact, I do." Jake pulled out the chair for her and grabbed her order from the pickup counter. "And good for you, by the way."

He'd just admitted to being miserable. "Good for me?"

"For not saying you're fine. You aren't. You couldn't be."

No one else had put it quite so bluntly. "I'm dying here." Jake cringed, the poignancy of what he'd just said hitting him. "Dying" couldn't be a regular word to him ever again. Or Cole. Her tilted, sad smile told him she understood. "I mean, it's *so* hard. How did you ever manage to keep it together in front of your girls?" He wrapped his hands around the extra-large coffee as if it could hold him to the table. "I feel like I need to be alone for eight weeks, and instead I've got a five-year-old on me every moment. I've got to show him how to do this and I have no idea how to do it myself."

"Jake, there isn't a right way to do this. It's different for everybody. It's different every day. There are still days where it comes up from behind and I feel knocked over."

"Really?" She seemed so together all the time. It probably would have been better not to sound so surprised.

She laughed at his astonishment. "Really. Even with all the blessings I have now. Even with Wyatt."

He found that incredible. "I'm swamped. I'm still mad. I feel like when we find whoever did this, I'll do things

Cole should never see." He couldn't believe he'd just let that thought out. His need for revenge made him a terrible person, didn't it? Who would tend to Cole if he let his anger get the best of him?

"I don't think you will."

He wasn't quite sure where all the certainty in her voice came from—Marilyn didn't know him well. "How do you know that?"

"Because you're worried that you could. And you seem to have quite a few people who care enough about you to catch you if you start to fall. That makes all the difference in the world, you know."

Her words stifled any reply Jake could make.

"Remember all the stuff in the old 'Goin' on a Bear Hunt' song?"

Jake looked at her, puzzled as he recited, "Can't go over it, can't go under it…" Until he saw her point as they both said, "Can't go around it, gotta go through it."

She sighed. "I know you want a secret tactic, or a shortcut, or just a way to know you're on the right track. I would have given anything for one."

"So there isn't one?" Jake couldn't tell if that made him feel better or worse.

"Only one that I know of."

"Which is…?"

"People around you. The ones who can remind you you're doing okay." Marilyn moved her coffee cup closer. "Some days that might be Cole, you know. Some days the girls would come up and put their arms around me just because they knew I was sad. Or because they were sad. So we let ourselves be sad together."

Jake thought about the moments back at the house before the nativity where Cole had buried his head in Jake's chest and they'd both missed Natalie so much it felt like the whole world broke open.

"But we let ourselves be happy, too. Being happy now doesn't mean you or Cole miss Natalie less."

Emma's Happy and Sad List. It was a simple little thing, but it seemed to navigate the way forward. *She* seemed to navigate his whole way forward. He was ready to pull her past the boundary she'd felt compelled to draw. He'd tell her what he really felt and convince her not to bow to the Norma Bintons of the world. Suddenly nothing else in his world felt as urgent as doing just that.

It was Christmastime, after all. The season of wonder. If not now, when else? Maybe being honest with Emma about his feelings was the way to all the clarity he was seeking. He was certain she felt the same about him. It had been all over her face last night.

Jake picked up the pair of coffees. "Thanks."

Marilyn watched him rise. "I'm not sure I did much."

"Oh, you did," he replied. "You did tons, believe me."

Coffees in hand, Jake walked back to the Chamber office to finish his work and recruit his partner as a last-minute babysitter so Jake could make a very important appearance at Emma's house that night.

Chapter Sixteen

Emma's whole body had been frozen for an hour in a kind of shock as she sat at her kitchen table. The sun had gone down, but she hadn't been able to move since the moment she'd pulled out the contents of her mailbox after coming home from Cole's house. *I'm wrong*, she told herself as she stared at the postcard. *I'm letting my fear get the best of my imagination. It can't be. But oh, help me, Lord, what if it is?*

The wind rattled the branches against her kitchen window, sounding like fingers clawing to get inside the house. Emma shut her eyes against the dizzy and slightly ill sensation that overtook her at the illustration. Taking a deep breath, she forced herself to look at the landscape depicted on the card, desperate to find reasons that it wasn't what she feared. Instead, another look—it must have been her fiftieth—only confirmed her first reaction.

It was entirely possible this drawing was of Natalie and Kurt's accident scene.

No, not entirely possible, it was probable. Certain, even, although she refused to let herself come to that horrid conclusion. She had to be wrong.

She also had to do something. But what? The fallout from every choice of action was so terrible she couldn't decide between them. Go to Jake? To Pastor? To the police? The notion that Sam was capable of something violent had been hounding her, pricking at her conscience and invading her dreams since the "I've done something" card arrived.

Sam had hated red cars since one had caused their mother's accident. Jake had said Chief Perkins told him they felt the shots were at "something" but not at Natalie and Kurt in particular. They had been driving a red minivan. The postcards all had red smears and lines. It all added up with hideous undeniability.

The fact that she hadn't been brave enough to say anything before this just made everything worse. Right at this moment, Emma couldn't even be certain her silence wasn't a crime in itself.

The knock on her back door made Emma startle out of her chair. She considered switching off the light and pretending not to be home. She wasn't ready to talk to anyone. In fact, the urge to get in her car and run away rose up with childish insistence.

The knock sounded again. "Emma?" came Jake's voice. "C'mon, Emma, let me in, please?"

Jake. She'd just left him minutes—no, wait, it had been hours—ago. He hadn't mentioned anything about coming over. How could Jake Sanders be at her door at this awful moment? Dread pulsed through her, cruel and cold.

I can't do this. I can't.

"I need to talk to you," Jake insisted through the door. "I know you want to be careful about this, but please, Emma, let me say what I came to say."

Jake was here to pick up where Zosia had interrupted.

She'd half expected it, defiant and persistent as he was about everything. He'd had a strange, insistent manner about him this afternoon, and now she knew why. He'd been planning to come here all day—after all, he'd have to have arranged for someone to watch Cole if he wanted any privacy.

He had no idea what had changed, how things could never be between them no matter what feelings they had come close to admitting last night.

She heard a soft thump, and she pictured Jake with his hands pressed up against her door. "Emma, don't do this," he said through the thick wood. "Hear me out. I'm not leaving."

Slowly, Emma rose and walked to the door. Her life was about to fall apart right in front of her. A shocked hollowness filled her chest as she put her hands to the latch. She opened the door to the sight of Jake standing in the light of her kitchen doorway, the wind tossing his hair and snow swirling around him.

How odd to notice how intense and strong he looked at that moment, how the power of his eyes sank right through her. He'd never look at her like that again. Not after he knew.

He stepped into her house, not bothering to brush the snow off his coat before grabbing her hand. That was Jake, all bold confidence. "I know you're worried about what…" He stopped, taking in her expression. "Wait… what's wrong?"

Everything was wrong. *How could You, Lord? How could You let him show up here, now?* Fear pushed every word from Emma's thoughts.

"What?" he repeated. The concern in his words broke her heart.

She kept trying to force even one syllable out, but there seemed to be nowhere safe to start.

Jake misread her silence. "Okay, I should have called first, I get that. But I wasn't sure you'd let me come and I don't want to say any of this over the phone or in front of Cole."

A gust of wind sent Sam's cards flying in all directions off the table, a cascade of black and white...and red. Emma's blood froze.

"Oops. I'll get those." Jake stooped to pick them back up.

She gasped, unable to stop the useless impulse to snatch them back and hide them from Jake's peering eyes. She tried to step in between Jake and the cards, but only bumped into him instead.

They both stared at the cards. Scattered on the floor like that, Sam's artwork no longer looked like an attempt to reach out. They looked like the scrawls of a madman. Jake stopped midreach, his hand still extended to gather the cards. "Are those from your brother?"

She couldn't seem to choke a single word out. Emma watched Jake's gaze settle on the card closest to his feet. It was the one that said, "I've done something." Why hadn't she hidden them? Why hadn't she locked them away in the farthest corner of her closet? Burned them, even?

The change in Jake's expression was like watching a wildfire begin. The destruction kindled and spread without any hope of being stopped. "Are they *all* from Sam?"

Any shred of hope she had left evaporated as she managed to say, "Yes." Emma stooped to gather them. Even now, even lost as the cause was, she wanted to scramble and clutch them all away from his view. Her hands wouldn't move fast enough. All of her felt pinned by the one card still sitting on the table, the one with the drawing of the overpass.

Emma watched Jake's gaze shift to that card, take in the detailed, artful depiction of Natalie's accident scene. The red smear—the only element every card shared no matter the landscape—now looked brutal and bloody. All the red marks no longer looked anything but gruesome. If the last card had scared her before, it horrified her now. She stopped trying to hide them. There was no point to that now.

Jake crouched over the table, his breath coming in short bursts. "That's…"

"It's just a drawing." What a frantic, foolish thing to say. Even she no longer believed that, no matter how much she had tried to convince herself otherwise.

"What are these?" he demanded again, louder this time. His whole demeanor had transformed in the handful of seconds since he'd come into the kitchen. His eyes no longer held the enthralling intensity she was finding hard to resist. Now they showed the rage that had been simmering just under Jake's skin all these weeks. A fury threatening to boil over. The kitchen door blew shut behind them, and they barely noticed. "How long have these been coming to you?"

"A while now."

Jake just stared at the cards, his eyes wide and full of hurt.

"I hadn't heard from him in months," she tried to explain. "Then all of a sudden these started coming. I told you about it." The floor seemed to tilt and crumble underneath her like a landslide.

"Not this," Jake said as he stared harder at the cards. "You didn't say anything about all these." He turned to look at her, and the darkness in his expression turned Emma's blood to ice. In that moment, Emma heard the delicate notes of a Christmas carol coming from the speaker behind them. She hadn't even realized the holiday music she'd turned on when she got home was still playing. How ironic that a song of peace and joy was the soundtrack to the unraveling of her life.

She didn't want to believe she'd made a horrible mistake by not saying something earlier. She wanted to be the kind of person who believed the best about her brother, who gave him every chance to…to what? Heal? Reconcile? Make her feel better about her own weak choice?

Emma knew the moment Jake's temper got the best of him. It was like the air snapped between them, and their connection broke in a way that couldn't be repaired. Exactly as she'd known it would.

He glared at Emma. In all his bitter outbursts, she'd never seen his eyes burn like this. At her. "Why didn't you say something?" It was more accusation than question.

"This one just arrived. I… I wasn't sure."

"So you waited until you were sure, is that it?" His words were sharp and hurtful.

"I couldn't be certain." She tried to match the strength of his tone, frustrated that she couldn't quite do it. Jake's personality was so large, so powerful. It was part of why she found him so attractive, but it also frightened her. She could be swallowed up by a presence of that size and charisma.

"But you had suspicions. Look at these. You can't tell me you didn't look at these and have some hint."

That wasn't fair. "I knew something was wrong, but not this. And would you make an accusation like that if you weren't sure? Absolutely, positively sure?" Emma waved the final postcard as if it were a shield to defend Sam. But both were flimsy.

Jake threw his hands up and walked away as if he couldn't bear to look at her. He began to pace her small kitchen, his temper apparently on the verge of exploding. "I deserved to know. How could you even think to keep this from me?" He pivoted and resumed his glare. "You know how hard they were looking for leads. That card is evidence, Emma."

"Only to you," she retorted. "To me it's just a postcard from Sam. And the way you're acting right now? That's exactly why I didn't say anything."

That wasn't true. She hadn't said anything because somewhere in her heart she suspected the postcards did condemn Sam to something terrible. But this? Kurt and Natalie? It filled her with fear that she'd somehow let him fall to this by giving up on him.

Jake walked over and grabbed the postcard from her hands, thrusting it in front of her face in a way that made her back up against the counter. "You see it. You see what this is, don't you?" He shook the card. "Look at the red. Nat's car was red. You got all weird when I mentioned it earlier. You can't tell me you don't see it."

It had been ridiculous to deny what the illustration was. She didn't want to see it, of course, but Jake was right; there was no denying the picture was of the overpass where the accident took place. "We don't know," she insisted without any strength behind the words. However horrifying the possibility, however crazy the odds were, however cruel it felt for their lives to be slammed together in this terrible new way, it had happened.

Sam. Kurt. Natalie. This stretched beyond any notion

she had of God's kindness or mercy. Not after what she'd come to feel for Jake and for Cole.

Deep underneath his anger, Jake was wrestling with it, too. "I… I don't…it…" Disconnected words tumbled out of him. The unthinkable clash of what they felt with what they'd just learned looked as if it was tearing Jake in two just as much as it had her. He paced the kitchen again, his hands flat against his chest, as if he had to physically hold himself together. It wasn't any different from how she felt. "Life falling apart" had seemed like such a dramatic phrase until this moment, when Emma's only thought was how completely her life *was* falling apart.

Jake stopped pacing. He'd reached some thought, and Emma found herself afraid of what that thought was. How many times had he made some comment about not being able to restrain his desire for revenge if he ever discovered who had taken Natalie's life?

When he turned to look at her, the former fire in his eyes had crystallized into a cold, hard determination. "Where is he?" He ground the words out through clenched teeth.

"I don't know." The three words let loose her tears, a million thoughts piled up behind the admission. She truly didn't know. She didn't know how to even begin to try to find Sam. Or what might await him if she did. Emma felt her spine ice over as it dawned on her how much she no longer knew about Sam. She used to see her brother so clearly in his artwork. There was only a glimpse of him in the angry, disjointed drawings. What if he had done this? He'd been out of touch for months— what if this wasn't the only thing he'd done? "He's never let me know."

She looked up to meet Jake's eyes, a helpless, drowning sensation filling her as if she'd been swept up into a rushing river. "Find him," he said, his voice low and cold.

That's what she had to do. There was no denying or hiding it now. Sam had to be found. The fallout from that—for him or for her—was no longer up to her. "How?" She didn't even bother to wipe the tears wetting her cheeks.

"We take the cards to Perkins." Jake started toward the cards.

Emma beat him to them, needing to gather them up herself. She frantically stacked them in a pile, watching as a tear dropped on the *M* in *SAM* on the one signed card, blurring it. In a flash of panic, she wondered if she'd ever see them again once they took them to the police.

"They'll do an APB or something," Jake continued from behind her. "The trouble was they didn't know who they were looking for. Now they do. They've got to have a way to find him."

"Yes." Sam had to be found.

"Have you got a photo of him around here somewhere?"

Emma's mind raced to the only photo of Sam in her home. The only one she'd wanted to keep because it was the only one where he was smiling. He looked so lost and angry in the others.

Without a word she walked into her bedroom and slid open the nightstand drawer. Jake did not follow her. She found and opened the little leather folding wallet-style frame that held a sunny snapshot of her and Sam on the steps of his group home two years ago. The face was only an echo of the man she'd visited this past spring. Any happiness, what there was left of it, had leaked out of him like water out of a jar too cracked to hold it in. Sam was broken. But was he broken enough to have fired those shots? It loomed both impossible and altogether too possible at the same time.

"I'll drive if you want."

The small, reluctant kindness only made it all worse. "No," Emma replied, sliding the photo and the cards into her handbag. She didn't bother with a coat or even turning off the Christmas music still coming from the player in the living room. "I'll drive myself."

It was nine o'clock in the evening in the Main Street police station, but it felt like two in the morning in the middle of nowhere. The only clear thought in Jake's brain was gratitude that he'd arranged for Bo and Toni to watch Cole. Cole should never be witness to what was going on right now. It would take a dozen years for him to find the right words to explain what just happened.

Emma looked lost and frightened, but his own anger threw up a wall between the two of them Jake couldn't hope to scale. She'd known. He couldn't believe she hadn't put it together the way it seemed too clear to him. And all this time he'd been going crazy looking for leads and praying for clues.

"I'm going to need to keep these," Chief Perkins said gently. Jake watched Emma wince as the chief slid Sam's stack of cards into a plastic evidence bag.

"I know." Emma's tone cut into Jake's heart a bit, but not enough to let him say anything. He should be the bigger man and show some compassion here, but it just wasn't possible.

"Do you have any idea, even the slightest hint, where he might be now?" Perkins asked.

"He's never given me any way to contact him." Her

voice wavered. "Believe me, I would tell you if I knew any way, but I don't."

"But you can find him, can't you?" Jake demanded. He was boiling with the urge to hunt Sam down, and that wasn't leaving any room for polite tones.

"It certainly makes it easier to know who we're looking for. But Sam doesn't have prints in the system, nor is the gun registered to his name." The chief nodded toward the cards now encased in plastic. "Those are incriminating, but they're not a confession. We can't be certain Sam did this."

Says you! Jake wanted to yell. He was on the verge of losing control. Tonight had made a mess of everything he had planned, and he was losing the battle to keep a lid on his storm of feelings.

Emma looked at him, and he knew he should say something. A better man would find a way to be kind, or at least understanding. She clearly found the idea of Sam's guilt as horrific as he did. She was hurting as badly as he was, if not worse. Still, he couldn't speak. If he opened his mouth, the torrent of angry, hurtful words would be unstoppable and there was enough pain in the room as it was.

This is beyond me and You know it! he shouted silently at God. Twists like this didn't happen in real life. The odds of his life colliding with Emma's and taking down so many hearts in the fallout seemed impossible. An epically, utterly destroyed Christmas.

"What else do you need me to do?" Emma asked in a voice so weary it almost got through to Jake. Almost. He realized he'd been gripping the arms of his chair so tightly his wrists had started aching. Every part of him—inside and out—was aching.

"Let us do our job. We'll do our best to bring Sam in without incident, but I think you should be ready for the possibility that your brother may be…violent…right now."

Jake watched Emma flinch at Perkins's reluctant choice of words. *Say something*, a small, insistent corner of his heart pleaded.

"That goes for you, too," Perkins said to him, his words taking on a warning tone. "Let us do our job. Emotions are running high here. Let's not make a bad situation worse." Then, as if he knew it was the one thing to keep Jake in line, the chief added, "Cole is watching you."

Cole. His actions now would have a lasting impact on Cole. *Get it together, man.* Jake liked to think he wasn't foolish enough to go off looking for Sam Mullins. But that didn't mean the urge to do it didn't simmer just under his skin. He tried to take Perkins's warning to heart. *Be the better man. No matter what it takes.* And right now it felt like it was going to take everything he had. *It's for Cole. He's worth it.*

"I'd like to go home now," Emma said, rising slowly.

"Of course. If you hear anything, or think of anything else that may help us find Sam, you've got my number. The faster we find him, the faster we can make sure this doesn't get any worse."

How on earth could it get any worse? Jake wondered. Christmas Eve was two days away. Everything was already worse beyond comprehension.

Jake watched Perkins walk Emma to the door, feeling like all the better, hopeful parts of him left in her wake.

Chapter Seventeen

Barely a day had gone by when Emma pulled open her front door early Wednesday morning to see Zosia, Pastor Newton and Chief Perkins standing on her front steps. The knot that had been twisting in her stomach tightened like a vise. There could be only one reason the three of them were here.

Sam.

The moment should have felt huge or dramatic. She waited for a wave of—what? Dread? Worry? But there was nothing. Instead, it felt more like snuffing a candle out—quick, silent and leaving only a wisp of empty smoke behind.

Chief Perkins removed his hat and looked at her with kind eyes. "May we come in?"

Her house was a mess, but it didn't matter. She was a mess, come to think of it, but that didn't matter, either. There was no point in making this moment about anything other than the delivery of whatever terrible news they'd come to relay. And it was terrible. She could see it on all of their faces.

"How about we sit down?" Pastor Newton said. He

was using the voice she'd heard him use to console church members. What could be worse than Sam being accused of Natalie and Kurt's deaths?

Zosia, without asking, went into the kitchen and put the teakettle on. Pastor Newton sat next to her while Chief Perkins took the chair opposite. Everyone was being so quiet and careful. The air felt thick and fragile at the same time.

Chief Perkins held his hat in his hands. "I want to let you know that we've located Sam. He was just off the state highway."

Emma was shocked at how close Sam was. How was that even possible? What twist of his mind kept him that close but so deliberately out of touch? With an odd, disconnected clarity, Emma recognized the highway Chief Perkins named as the one Kurt and Natalie had been traveling. But that was hours from some of the postmarks on the cards.

There was something everyone wasn't saying. Zosia sat down on the other side of Emma and took her hand.

"Emma," Pastor Newton said gently. "I'm afraid I have difficult news."

She'd known that whenever they found Sam and brought him in, things would be difficult. It would all get very public, sad and ugly. She no longer hoped that Sam hadn't been the one firing shots on the overpass. Somewhere in the past two days the certainty that it had been him settled on her like a heavy cloak, thick and suffocating.

"Emma," Pastor Newton continued, "Sam took his own life."

The room hung still for a moment, then began to blur around her. She'd been prepared for bad news, but not this. Gone? Sam? By his own hand? It couldn't be. "I'm so sorry," came Zosia's voice, but it sounded so far away. There were more words, insistent and gentle tones, but none of it pushed through the roar of what she'd just heard. Sam had died. Sam had killed himself.

"On Monday we received a report of someone living out in the woods," said the chief. "Turns out he matched Sam's description. But as we were heading out last night to investigate, we got another call…"

Living outside? On a mountainside in a Colorado December? The painful image of Sam shivering in the cold, alone and tortured by the emotions he never could seem to control, made her wobble.

"How?" But really, what did it matter?

Chief Perkins lowered his eyes to the floor. "The overpass, I'm afraid."

He didn't say "an" overpass. He said "the" overpass. No one needed to explain the distinction.

Suddenly she was choking and crying at the same time. Sam had died alone and desperate. She'd cut him off; she'd severed the tie that might have let him hang on. Emma tried to gulp in air, unable to stop the drowning sensation threatening to swallow her. She'd told herself before there was no hope for Sam, but now there truly was no hope.

"There's more," Pastor Newton said as Zosia gripped Emma's hand tight.

More? How could there be more? Who could stand more?

"There was a journal of sorts in a nearby tent. Drawings and writings. It's hard to piece together, just like the cards. But it did enable us to match the writing since Sam had written on some of the cards."

Emma knew where this was leading. "I've done something" flooded her vision in Sam's sprawling, angular letters. She knew what that something was. She couldn't even bring herself to put it into words. She could barely lift her gaze to the chief's. He nodded only once.

She'd heard people say that they'd "unraveled" or "gone to pieces." This was so much worse than that. It was as if she'd disintegrated, crumbled out of existence into something that only looked like Emma Mullins. Even surrounded by people who cared about her, she felt inconceivably alone.

"It's awful," Zosia said, her voice filled with compassionate tears. "I'm so sorry for you to lose your brother this way." She wrapped both of her hands around Emma's. "*Kochanie*, I don't understand why you didn't share this burden with us. Why you felt you had to go through such an awful thing alone."

Maybe, in that way, she was no different from Sam. Close but keeping out of touch. Maybe there had never been any real hope for either of them all these years. The loathsome truth that she'd been ashamed of Sam pressed mercilessly against her heart.

"When can I…see…him?" Her voice shook at the weight of hopelessness in her question, but she had so many things to say to Sam. Even if he couldn't hear them, Emma felt like she'd simply break apart if she didn't get the chance to say them. So much could never get better. So much was gone for good. Forever—or this side of Heaven, at least.

"Are you sure you want to do that?" Pastor Newton asked gently.

"You need someone to confirm it's him, don't you?" Who else would? Her father could never come quickly enough—if he came at all. There had really only been her and Sam in their world, and now there was only her.

"Not in this case. And I'm not sure I'd advise it."

She had to. If there was any hope of ever coming to peace with this—and who knew if that would ever be possible—she had to. God would just have to hold her up long enough to do this one thing. The fact that it would break her couldn't matter. She was, in this case and perhaps always, her brother's keeper. If she'd done a terrible job of it before, this was her last chance to take care of him now.

"I want to see him. I know it will be hard." A fresh wave of tears overtook her. "But I think it will be harder not to."

"I'll come with you," Zosia said, tightening her grip on Emma's hand.

"That's kind, but I think this is something I have to do on my own."

"Are you sure?" Pastor Newton pressed again. "There's no reason for you to face this alone."

"Yes, there is," Emma replied.

No one asked her to explain why.

"I don't wanna go to Gam's!"

Cole was pitching another fit worthy of a two-year-old. The temper tantrum he'd thrown this morning had taxed Jake to the limits of his patience. Much to his own horror, the words "Because I said so!" had even left his mouth. Christmas Eve was turning out to be a first-class disaster.

Which made it easy to just give in and flee that disaster. After all, leaving couldn't make it worse—it was already terrible. The past twenty-four hours convinced

Jake he couldn't stay in Wander Canyon. Not this Christmas. Staying was flat-out impossible.

Bo had called twice, but Jake didn't pick up. No amount of talking to anyone would fix this, and why ruin anyone else's Christmas Eve with his own personal shrapnel? If Bo got nosy and showed up, Jake couldn't be sure he wouldn't simply refuse to answer the door. He was in that black a mood. *Grinch.*

He felt like the biggest Grinch in history, in fact, insisting against Cole's tears and whining that they were going to Sarah's. The honest truth was that Jake was beyond his capacity to cope, whether Cole liked it or not. Escape felt like the only thing that would keep him upright and breathing.

Not that escape was easy. When he'd called Sarah yesterday to tell her what had happened and why he was coming—using the vaguest possible terms even out of Cole's earshot, which proved nearly an impossible trick in itself—she'd sobbed into the phone.

"Come. Lord have mercy, just come," she'd said. "We'll find a way to make it work." Even in a cast and a walker, Sarah was a better parent to Cole than he could ever hope to be.

His nephew had cried himself into a fitful nap rolled up on his bed. On the morning of Christmas Eve. Things seemed to be spiraling downward out of his control. *It'll be better there*, Jake told himself over and over as he quietly packed a suitcase for Cole and himself. Christmas with Sarah and her friends at a retirement community would probably be drab and boring, but right now every single square inch of Wander Canyon seemed to bring him too much pain to care.

Jake peeked into Cole's room to check on the little

guy and ended up leaning brokenhearted against the door frame, watching Cole's restless sleep. The little boy clutched his stuffed turtle close and sucked his thumb. *How will I ever tell him? How can I ever find the words to say that Emma's brother took his mom and dad from him?* It might be the coward's way out, but leaving was the only thing Jake could think of to do. At this moment, he couldn't even be sure he'd find it in himself to come back. Ever. *I'm sorry, buddy.* There was too much damage everywhere he looked to even try to stomach Christmas. He wasn't any kind of parent. He was just a lost uncle bumbling his way through this mother lode of tragedy and pain.

Staring at Cole's round cheeks, Jake surrendered to the thought he'd tried to hide from since leaving the chief's office. *How could You let this happen, Lord? In what world is this even close to fair? I'm ready to explode. I've lost Nat, Emma's beyond me, and if You want to know the truth, I'm having trouble hanging on to You. There's no faith left in here. I'm empty.*

Jake shut the door quietly and tried to finish gathering their things. It felt like moving through mud, every action taking more strength than he had. The whole thing was the stuff of nightmares—a burn of urgency exacerbated by a wild inability to move. He probably didn't have half of what he needed, but Jake piled up the bags and walked toward the garage door anyway. He'd leave the moment Cole woke up. Maybe he'd even tuck him in the car while he was still asleep.

The sight outside the house's front window stopped him cold.

There, in the snow next to a cheery snowman she'd built with Cole earlier that week, stood Emma.

Small and shivering, she looked as childlike as Cole—were it not for the mountain of pain in her eyes. She looked completely undone. As utterly wrecked as Jake was, and that was saying something.

There, lit by the clear sunlight that had always made Wander Canyon sparkle in the winter, was the last person Jake wanted to see. And at the same time, the only person he wanted to see. Emma had been the only person he'd ever thought could fix him, fix this. And yet since Monday, he'd been unable to stop the stream of pain and blame his heart threw at her. He knew it was illogical. He knew she was hurting as much as he was. And still, Emma could be a thousand miles away and not feel more distant from him than she was now, standing on the lawn.

He opened the door, barely feeling the chilly wind that swept in around him. She'd been crying, still was by the swipe of her bright yellow mitten against one cheek. It brought back the memory of wiping her tears away in the church classroom, and Jake discovered that his heart could break into even more pieces than it already had.

She walked toward him, another small sob heaving her chest. Somewhere deep down he found the grace to keep the door open. She moved up onto the front steps of the house but made no effort to come inside.

"Sam." She said only that word, but the tears behind it told him they'd found her brother. Jake couldn't decide if the speed of that made it better or worse. Perhaps it was neither, just over. Natalie and Kurt's killer would meet his justice.

"They found him," he said. He waited for the words to sink in, to calm the storm in his chest. No closure, no sense of justice or finality came. The thing he'd craved for weeks was finally here, and it did nothing to ease his pain.

"Jake," she said, losing her battle to keep the tears at bay. "He's…he's dead." The words seemed to claw their way out of her, tearing her in half right in front of his eyes.

Sam was dead. Jake's mind brought up the image of a deadly standoff, a wild man shouting and surrounded by police. Numb. That was the only thing he felt about her news—hollow and numb.

Until she gulped out, "He…he did it himself."

Something in him fell to pieces. A crash like an avalanche hit him, knocking the air out of his lungs. It wasn't a conscious choice to pull her into the house. The pain in his heart simply pushed aside the rage and reached out to the pain in hers.

"He's gone," she wailed as she stumbled inside. "He's gone."

Jake's heart called instantly back to the moment he'd said those exact words into the night air. *She's gone.* The details of her crash with Kurt were painful enough, but nothing surmounted the raw anguish of Natalie being *gone*.

It should have been a force of will, a decision to be that "better man" that opened his arms, but it wasn't. It was the instant, overwhelming surrender to the fact that the only way they could ever hope to survive this terrible mess was together. Jake wasn't sure if he fell into her or if she fell into him. It seemed astounding that they both didn't crumple to the floor, that they somehow managed to hold each other upright.

"He killed Natalie and Kurt and then he killed himself." She wept into his chest. "He was so lost. So lost and I let him go. I should have stuck by him. I should have tried harder. I should have stopped him before..." Her words dissolved into a racking sob that brought tears to Jake's own eyes.

She looked up at him, helpless and lost. "I know you hate me, but I couldn't...no one else... I had to see you... I need you." The desperate tone of those last words tore down the wall of pain and let the black storm empty out from where it had built up inside.

"I don't hate you." He felt tears heat his own face. "I don't hate you," he repeated, as much for himself as for her. The truth of those words pulled the wall all the way down. In the space behind all that dissipated anger was another, more powerful truth. He took her face in his hands. "I love you."

Her eyes widened at the impossibility of that statement. Jake was as startled as she was, stunned by the admission even he hadn't seen coming.

"You do?" It seemed as hard for her to get her mind around the idea as it was for him.

"Yeah," he admitted, shaking his head. "As a matter of fact, it's the only thing that makes any sense in all of this." Wasn't it? Wasn't it the only thing that made any of this bearable?

She stared at him, stunned and blinking. Her face reflected the "Is this really happening?" question currently taking over his own heart. He felt the nonstop press of anger seep out of his body, and the sensation of relief nearly buckled his knees.

With one exception. While he had a pretty good guess, the need to know surged up to tighten his chest. "You... um...any chance you feel the same way?"

Without a word, Emma leaned up toward him and

kissed him. Jake felt himself melt against her, desperate to hold on to this new, most precious thing God had been kind enough to grant him. He felt the grip of her arms and the moisture of her tearful cheeks. Her kiss swept the black storm far away, replacing it with the taste of light and hope. He loved her. Maybe he'd even loved her from the beginning. And as huge as the pile of sorry circumstances all around them was, this one truth held it all at bay.

"I love you," he said again, just because it felt like waking back up to life again to say it. She smiled—a wet, wobbly, astonished smile Jake knew would stick in his heart forever. He pulled her even closer, and the feeling of her head against his chest was perfection. "What do you know?" he said into the adorable tumble of her hair. "Love really is the answer." She laughed. Softly, wearily, but it fluttered against him in a way that made it hard to breathe. Or perhaps it made breath possible again.

Emma pulled back just enough to look into his eyes. "I was afraid to love you."

Fear robbed so many good things from life. He brushed a lock of hair from her eyes. The action made him want to take care of her forever. A gushy thought to be sure, but Jake found he didn't mind one bit. "And now?" he asked, needing to hear the words from her.

"I'm not afraid anymore. I love you."

If anyone had told him he could be happy this morning— maybe even happy ever again—he'd never have believed it. Jake kissed her then. Really, truly kissed her, as if she meant everything to him. Because she did. She was his path through this valley, the light to his wiser nature, the only way for it all to make sense. He heard the astonishment in her breath and knew it was the same for her.

"It's all still terrible…well, except for this," she said, tightening her arms around him.

"I know." She was right. None of the circumstances that had brought them together had changed. In fact, they had worsened. But there was this. There was love. One clear, brilliant thought popped into his head. "It's the whole Christmas thing, isn't it? One light of love in a messed-up world?"

"That's rather profound, Mr. Sanders."

Divine intervention, to be sure. He certainly couldn't claim much wisdom in his starstruck state. "Hey, sometimes I surprise even myself." He laughed—a laugh that felt so much lighter than he'd known in such a long time—but then grew serious. "I'm sorry," he said, making sure he looked into her eyes. "I shut you out and blamed you for my own anger. Forgive me."

Emma absolved him with the tenderest of kisses. Jake let himself be lost in it, wondrous as it was.

Until a tiny voice broke the moment. "Huh?"

Jake turned to find Cole, sleepy-eyed and still dragging his stuffed turtle, staring at them. His little brow furrowed. "Why are you kissing Miss Emma?" Cole clearly found the idea a little, well, icky.

Jake and Emma looked at each other, neither one ready with an answer to that question suitable for a five-year-old.

"It's Christmas Eve," Jake finally replied, deciding that answer made as much sense as any of the others he could have given.

Cole's face squished up in thought over that response, then he simply said, "Okay." After a moment's consideration, he asked, "Are we still going to Gam's?"

Emma looked at him in a panic, her eyes finding the pile of suitcases a few feet away.

"No, buddy. Change of plans. We're staying right here where we belong."

Chapter Eighteen

Candles filled the darkened sanctuary of Wander Canyon Community Church like tiny beams of hope. The familiar verses of "Silent Night" wafted around Emma as they filled the air. Wander Canyon felt still and sacred, wrapped this Christmas Eve in a picture-perfect blanket of snow and twinkling lights.

Cole lay stretched out on her and Jake's laps, having dozed off after the tumult of the day. Jake's arm was strong around her shoulders. Defiant, even, as if he dared all of Wander Canyon to utter one syllable of protest. There had been a few stares as they walked into the church as a trio, but she hadn't minded.

"Merry Christmas," Jake had said, planting his arm around Emma with astounding confidence as Norma Binton walked by to take her traditional place in a front pew. The old woman's mouth had practically come unhinged. "Think we ruined her Christmas?" Jake whispered with a wink.

"I hope not," Emma said as she watched Norma take up her place. She sat alone, as Carrie had gone back to Boulder to be with her own parents. Alone on Christmas

Eve. A surprising surge of sympathy rose up for the old woman. Maybe, when this was all over, she could find a way to befriend Old Biddy Binton. Wouldn't that shock the town?

When Bo and Toni had found them in the lobby before the service, Jake's hand declaratively clamped onto Emma's, the pair had simply smiled. "Well, look at you," Bo said to his partner.

"Yeah, look at me," Jake had said. Emma had discovered that this new happy Jake was even more handsome than the sadder and angry version. He would sweep her clean off her feet when they could be truly happy again.

Emma said a prayer of thankfulness that she'd thought *when* and not *if*. It stunned her still to think that happiness was possible in light of all that had happened. The hopeful candles glowing in the darkness were the perfect illustration of what this Christmas meant to her. The darkness wasn't gone, but it had been held back. The yuletide message of hope come to a broken world echoed deep in her soul. She truly felt "the dawn of redeeming grace" that was sung about in the song's lyrics. Christmas hadn't been ruined. It had been broken, strained, darkened in a way that would never fully lift, but Jake's love had redeemed it.

Emma let her head rest on Jake's shoulder, weary from the sleep she hadn't had and the day's grim tasks. She had called her father to give him the news, and they had both cried on the phone. They'd talked—stiffly, awkwardly— but they'd both made an effort. It wasn't a healing, but it was a start.

When Jake asked if she would spend an hour or two by the fire with him tonight after the service—"Someone's gotta help me hang the stockings by the chimney with care," he'd pleaded—nothing sounded more peaceful or perfect. She had spent past Christmas mornings alone or driving up to the group home to wrestle through a visit with Sam. The thought of spending tomorrow morning with Cole and Jake at Bo and Toni's house felt like a new beginning. A first small step into what she hoped would be a new life.

As the hymn closed, Emma looked up at Jake and silently mouthed, "I love you." Then, just because it was Christmas, she added, "Both of you," hoping he'd read her lips clearly enough.

He had. The glow in his eyes rivaled Wander Canyon's brightest stars. Their sparkle sang under her skin, sending warmth into even the weariest parts of her heart. Without a single care for who was watching, Jake leaned down, kissed her temple and then whispered, "Merry Christmas, my love."

There was a newer Christmas song—destined to be a favorite of hers—that proclaimed "hope was born this night."

Never had it been more true.

Cole burst through the door like the tornado of energy he was, yards ahead of Emma and her pile of bags. Since Emma's organizational skills had the upcoming Valentine's Day decorations already up at the preschool classroom, she and Cole had gone shopping together to get a head start on St. Patrick's Day decorations. Emma was proving to be outstanding in her new role as Director of the Wander Canyon Community Church Preschool.

Normally, Jake would have rushed out to help with the bags. Today, however, the element of surprise had to rank over chivalry.

"The squishy chairs came!" Cole called as he dashed into the kitchen.

"So I hear," Jake replied. Emma had texted him that she'd received word from Pastor Newton that three large and "squishy" chairs had been delivered to the church. They were the last pieces of the finished library to be put into place. Jake liked to think Nat had had a hand in the perfect timing of their arrival today.

"Cake!" his nephew cried with glee as he spied the cheery little green confection Jake had ordered from the Wander Canyon Bakery. Yvonne Walker was back from her maternity leave and had been glad to be in on today's scheme. After all, a guy couldn't trust just any baker to whip up the perfect turtle cake for this occasion. "For Valentine's?" Cole asked, working to get his mouth around the word. Tomorrow was Valentine's Day.

"Not exactly," Jake admitted. "It's green, after all."

"And Valentine's stuff is red," Cole agreed.

"But when has your Uncle Jake ever done what everyone else does?" Emma asked as she deposited the collection of bags on the counter. She smiled at Jake. They'd planned this little celebration, but she didn't know the half of it.

Cole shucked his jacket and climbed up on the chair to stare at the cake. "It's got turtles!"

Jake grinned. "It does indeed." He caught Emma's eyes and enjoyed the glow of her smile.

"What's it say?" his nephew asked. "I see a *G* and a *T*." The class had been working on alphabet letters all month.

Coming over to stand beside Cole, Jake pointed to the word that graced the top of the cake in bright yellow frosting. Surrounded, of course, by four green frosting turtles. "It says *Gotcha*!" The word caused an unexpected lump to rise in Jake's throat.

Cole scrunched his face up in puzzlement. "Whassat mean?"

"It means today is your Gotcha Day." Jake felt Emma take his hand behind Cole's back.

"Huh?"

"Today is the day I officially adopt you. I've always been your uncle, and I was your guardian for a while. As of today, I'm your new official dad. If that's okay with you, I mean."

For a second, Jake's pulse stilled while Cole pondered the idea. "S'okay with me," Cole said, as if it were as simple as that. Perhaps it was. "Can I have some cake now?"

"Absolutely," Jake said, feeling the final piece of his world slide into place. "Wouldn't have it any other way." With that, he carefully cut two slices, setting them on plates in front of Cole and himself.

"Hey," Emma teased even as she sniffed away a tear. "What about me?"

This had gone exactly according to plan. Jake reached over to another smaller box sitting on the counter behind him. "You don't get any of this cake."

Emma crossed her arms over her chest. "What do you mean by that?"

"You get *this* cake. Well, cupcake." He opened the box to reveal a frosted cupcake with the word *Gotcha* in red. And decorated with hearts, not turtles. "It's your Gotcha Day, too."

"Huh?" Emma echoed Cole's words and face. And then, as she realized his message, her whole face broke into the most delightful, hope-filled joy.

Jake lifted the cupcake out of its container to reveal

the blue velvet box sitting underneath. He set the cupcake down, picked up the box and opened it to show the
sparkling, heart-shaped diamond within.

He got down on one knee. "Emma Mullins, I want
this to be the day you join my family, too. I can't imagine doing any of this without you. Will you marry me—
well, Cole and me?"

Emma began to cry as she said, "Yes."

"Gotcha!" Cole wrapped his little arms around Emma
as Jake slid the ring onto her finger.

"Gotcha!" he repeated just before giving his bride-
to-be the world's most joyful kiss.

Epilogue

Cole ran in from the mailbox to show Gam. "Another one!" he shouted. "Another one's here!"

Gam set down her book and motioned for Cole to climb up on her lap. "Well now, let's take a look. Where do you suppose they are now?"

Cole held up the postcard. "There's a Z in it. And prickly plants."

Gam's fingers ran across the big blue letters on the picture side of the card. "Greetings from Arizona," she read. "Those are cactus plants."

"Cool," Cole said. "Read the other side."

Gam read him the message:

Dear Cole,
We are having fun on our honeymoon in the big red car. We miss you and hope you and Gam are having fun, too. It's hot and there are funny plants and lizards and tortoises, which are big, not-wet turtles. The highways are long and flat lots of the time. Next year we'll take a different trip, all three of us, okay?

We love you,
Dad and Emmom

Cole kissed the little heart Emmom drew at the bottom of every card the way he did every time.

Gam laughed. "How blessed you are to have two daddies and two mommies to love you. Did you come up with *Emmom*?"

He grinned. "Yep."

"Well, that's about as perfect as can be." She looked back at the picture. It did have a long, flat road on it, just like they said. "They're having fun, aren't they?" Gam asked. "Think how much more fun it will be when you get to go along on the next trip."

Cole looked at Gam. "What about you?"

Gam hugged him. "Oh, I think cross-country drives in red Chevy convertibles are a young person's game. Besides, I need to be here to get all the postcards you're going to send me, don't I?"

Cole had never thought about it that way. "You're right." You couldn't take a trip like that and not send a whole bunch of postcards to somebody.

Gam started to work her way out of the chair. "Let's go put this one on the map with the other cards. Then we can have a snack and feed your turtles."

He grinned. Gam always made the best snacks. "Sounds good to me."

* * * * *

*If you enjoyed this story,
be sure to check out
the other Wander Canyon books*

Their Wander Canyon Wish
Winning Back Her Heart

*And be sure to pick up
Allie Pleiter's previous miniseries,
Matrimony Valley*

His Surprise Son
Snowbound with the Best Man
Wander Canyon Courtship

*Find these and other great reads at
www.LoveInspired.com*

Dear Reader,

From the very first moment the carousel caught my eye, I've loved my visits to Wander Canyon. The characters feel like old friends, and my heart roots for their happiness (yes, even Norma Binton's!). I love stories where the imperfections and charm of a small town combine to show us how God's plan always unfolds in perfect wisdom. We don't often see it at first, but then, isn't that what friends and faith are for?

Emma and Jake face monumental hurdles in their journey back to the hope and joy each of them has lost. But in finding each other, they discover how love's pure light can fight back even the darkest of circumstances. It's my prayer that their story fuels your own hope in the redemption God has in store for whatever struggles you face. Hang on, dear reader, nothing is ever too big or too dark for God to redeem.

I'd love to hear how this story touched you. You can reach me at allie@alliepleiter.com, on Facebook, Twitter and Instagram, and through good old postal mail at P.O. Box 7026, Villa Park, IL 60181.

Blessings,
Allie

COMING NEXT MONTH FROM
Love Inspired

Available December 1, 2020

AN AMISH HOLIDAY COURTSHIP
by Emma Miller
Ready to find a husband at Christmastime, Ginger Stutzman has her sights set on the handsome new Amish bachelor in town. But she can't help but feel drawn to her boss, Eli Kutz, and his four children. Could the widower be her true perfect match?

A PRECIOUS CHRISTMAS GIFT
Redemption's Amish Legacies • by Patricia Johns
Determined to find a loving Amish family for her unborn child, Eve Shrock's convinced Noah Wiebe's brother and sister-in-law are a great fit. But when she starts falling for Noah, the best place for her baby might just be in her arms...with Noah at her side.

HIS HOLIDAY PRAYER
Hearts of Oklahoma • by Tina Radcliffe
Beginning a new job after the holidays is the change widower Tucker Rainbolt's been praying for. Before he and his twin girls can move, he must ensure his vet clinic partner, Jena Harper, can take over—and stay afloat. But could giving his heart to Jena be the fresh start he *really* needs?

CHRISTMAS IN A SNOWSTORM
The Calhoun Cowboys • by Lois Richer
Returning home to his Montana family ranch, journalist Sam Calhoun volunteers to run the local Christmas festival. But as he works with single mom Joy Grainger on the project, the last thing he expects is for her children to set their sights on making him their new dad...

THE TEXAN'S UNEXPECTED HOLIDAY
Cowboys of Diamondback Ranch • by Jolene Navarro
Driven to get her sister and baby niece out of a dangerous situation, Lexy Zapata takes a job near Damian De La Rosa's family's ranch and brings them with her. Now they can stay hidden through Christmas, and Lexy will start planning their next move...if she can ignore the way Damian pulls at her heart.

A DAUGHTER FOR CHRISTMAS
Triple Creek Cowboys • by Stephanie Dees
Moving into a cottage on Triple Creek Ranch to help her little girl, Alice, overcome a traumatic experience, single mom Eve Fallon doesn't count on rescuing grumpy rancher Tanner Cole as he struggles to plan a party for foster kids. Can she revive both Tanner's and Alice's Christmas spirit?

LICNM1120

Get 4 FREE REWARDS!

We'll send you 2 FREE Books plus 2 FREE Mystery Gifts.

Love Inspired books feature uplifting stories where faith helps guide you through life's challenges and discover the promise of a new beginning.

FREE
Value Over
$20